ORPHAN TRAIN TRIALS

HEARTS ON THE RAILS BOOK 2

RACHEL WESSON

CHAPTER 1

46TH ST, NEW YORK APRIL, 1894

Kathleen Collins read the letter from her sister Bridget quickly, greedily consuming all her news.

"Has Bridget listened to our advice to stay away from New York?"

Kathleen looked up at Lily's question. She hated upsetting this kind woman who had done so much to help her family. She shook her head. "She says they will be here in about two weeks. First, they are going to visit Doctor Powell and his wife, the people who adopted Sally."

"I wonder if they were able to help Sally's limp. She was such a lovely happy child with her beautiful smile." Lily sighed causing Kathleen to look up in concern.

"Kathleen, I admit to being torn. I am looking forward to seeing your sister again and congratulating her on her marriage, but I don't want to place her in danger."

"Lily, it's been almost a year since we left the factory. Surely, Mr. Oaks will have forgotten about Bridget now. He should have other things on his mind with the financial crash."

Lily smiled sadly. "You would think so, especially with over sixteen thousand businesses folding. Charlie said one in six men are now out of work. But, somehow, Mr. Oaks and his ilk tend to survive, perhaps thrive in difficult times like these. I heard from Inspector Pascal Griffin. Oaks is a man who never forgets, especially someone like Bridget."

Kathleen exchanged a glance with her friend, Bella. They knew how difficult life was in New York with the increased unemployment meaning more visitors to the sanctuary. Still, she hoped Inspector Griffin was wrong, although he wouldn't have got to such a senior level in the police force if he wasn't usually correct in these matters.

She was dying to see Bridget, she missed her and Annie and Liam. She also wanted to get to know her new brother-in-law better. Having only met him briefly when Annie and Liam joined the orphan train, she couldn't help but wonder what her vivacious older sister saw in such a stern, sad man. Yet Bridget was happy, more than happy. Her letters flowed with joy over her new role as an outplacement agent. Even when she wrote of the things that annoyed her, her tone was one of someone who believed in the work they were doing. She continually praised her husband Carl.

"Bridget won't be staying in New York for long, so she should be fine," Lily said, bending to reach the knitting by her chair. They were in her private sitting room taking advantage of some quiet time. Charlie was away with work and Lily had to wait for Mini Mike or Tommy to collect her to escort her home. Charlie had left strict instructions on the care his wife was to receive. Lily joked Charlie must think she was the first woman to have a child, but everyone knew he was just being careful. They had been married a long time, almost five years.

"How is Inspector Griffin?" Kathleen asked in a bid to change the conversation away from Oaks and danger. "The papers are full of stories about how the New York police department needs to be cleaned up."

"I think there are more criminals in the force than outside it," Bella said, not looking up from the sketch she was working on. Kathleen looked over her shoulder, trying to see the dress. Bella had a wonderful eye for detail. They used to take walks down to Fifth Avenue to view the dresses in the store windows. When they got back, Bella would take out her sketch pad and draw similar designs to those she had seen in the stores. She really was very clever.

"Bella, that's not true," Lily reprimanded gently.

Bella put her pencil down and looked Lily straight in the face. "Yes, it is, Lily. Every woman who comes here has a similar story about paying the police bribes, either in cash or favors." Bella's face turned various shades of pink, partly from anger at the injustices the women faced, and partly from embarrassment Kathleen surmised.

"Those men are supposed to protect every-one, but they don't care about the children in the tenements. They just lock them up."

"Bella, I know you are upset about young Dillon and Sammy being arrested, but they were caught in the act," Kathleen said gently. "You can't blame the police for picking them up."

"Can't I? Those kids had to do it, the gangs told them to. What would happen to them if they refused? The police are afraid of the East-mans and the Five Pointers."

The gangs ruled New York, that much was true, although there were police officers trying to fight back. But corruption was rife, and many law enforcers looked the other way depending on which gang was involved. There were rumors the government was going to do something to sort out the corruption but, as yet, nothing much had happened. But there were still some police who wore their uniform with pride and served their community as best they could.

"Bella, that's unfair. Inspector Griffin was talking about that very thing when he called to check on us over the weekend. He said there are moves being made to get the gang situation under control but, in the meantime, we have to be patient," Lily said, her tired tone making Kathleen wish Mini Mike or Tommy would come back to take Lily home.

"I'm sorry, Lily." Bella looked contrite, "I just can't bear the sight of those kids in the cells. I know they act all tough but putting children in with real criminals is just wrong." Bella pursed her lips together as she screwed her eyes shut. Not one tear escaped but Kathleen had seen her friend's eyes fill up. She squeezed her arm gently trying to show her she cared.

"Bella, you reminded me. I can't believe I forgot," Lily said, sitting straighter in the chair. "Being pregnant is making me forgetful. Father Nelson spoke to me yesterday about a group of orphaned children coming to us from a prison somewhere north of here," Lily explained.

"A prison?" Kathleen clarified.

"Yes. It is bad enough when youngsters like Sammy or Dillon get picked up and thrown in a cell for a night. But these children have been living in the prison. Their only crime is that of being poor and orphaned. The local authorities maintain it's because the orphanages are overflowing."

"You don't believe them?" Kathleen asked.

Lily picked up the teapot and poured more

tea into their cups. Lily sat back farther in her seat as if taking time to compose her thoughts.

"I believe the existing facilities are over-crowded, but that is not where the blame lies. Until our government views the needs of vulnerable children with the same importance as other issues, there will never be enough money or safe places for the people who need them most." Lily stopped talking, an apologetic look on her face. "Forgive me, girls. Charlie tells me not to get on my soap box."

"Nothing to apologize for," Kathleen said. "I wish there were more people who think like you do, Lily. I feel so bad for those we left behind in the tenements. When Mam was alive, she used to share what we had with the families who lived around us. Like Mrs. Fleming does."

"Speaking of Mrs. Fleming, would you like to come and visit her with me?" Lily asked. "I am going tomorrow night—Mini Mike and Tommy will be with us. I had a message to call on her last week but as I had a chill, Charlie ordered me to bed."

"Yes, please. I would love to see her," Kathleen answered. "Bella, would you like to come with us. Mrs. Fleming is such a lovely lady. Her husband, Dave, and children are nice too. They were very good to us when my mam died." Kathleen had been thrilled Bella had opened up so much and become a close friend. She would never replace Bridget in her affections, but she had helped her through a very lonely time. She wanted Bella to meet Mrs. Fleming who did so much work in the community helping families to help themselves.

Bella looked up from her sketching, "Yes, please."

"That's settled then," Lily said, smiling at Bella. Kathleen knew Lily wanted to get Bella to be more trusting of people. To see that not everyone was as horrible as the people who had mistreated her when she was younger.

"Kathleen, can you ask Cook to bake a few more batches of cookies? They always disappear quickly. We'll need some blankets and some clothes as well. You know the drill by now," Lily said, smiling at Kathleen, making her feel warm inside. Since Bridget had left, Kathleen had gone out with Lily on her rounds visiting those families who couldn't, or wouldn't, come to the sanctuary. She couldn't say she enjoyed going back to the tenements. She didn't. There was no comparison between her current home and the overcrowded, wretched squalor she had once lived. She was so grateful Lily had taken her family in.

"I'll go now and get organized. Thank you, Lily." She stood and gathered the cups to take the tray with her. Bella stood to answer the door, they all recognized Tommy's knock.

"Evening, ladies." Tommy acknowledged them. "Are you ready to go home, Miss Lily?"

"Yes, thank you, Tommy." Lily beamed at her friend and protector. "Wait, Kathleen, what about Maura? Would she like to come with us?"

Kathleen didn't look at Lily but stared at a

point above her head. Embarrassed at her sister's behavior, she wasn't sure if Lily knew of the latest problems Maura had caused. Bella didn't make any comment. Kathleen thought it was loyal of her not to complain to Lily about how badly Maura had treated her over the last month in particular.

"Why don't you ask Maura?" Lily asked when Kathleen didn't respond. "She may find it good to get out of the sanctuary and back into the real world if only for a few hours."

Kathleen wasn't at all sure Maura would say yes, so she just kept quiet.

CHAPTER 2

NEW YORK

Kathleen entered the bedroom she and Maura now shared. They had moved to the smaller space when the others had left for Riverside Springs. Her elder sister didn't glance at her as she came in, let alone say anything. Obviously, she was in another one of her moods.

"Are you going out again, Maura?" Kathleen asked, wondering how her sister funded all her trips. Although they had jobs in the sanctuary, their wages were quite low.

"What's it to do with you? You're not my keeper."

"I am going to see Mrs. Fleming with Lily and Bella tomorrow evening. I thought you might like to come with us."

"No, thanks," Maura said as she picked up her hat and purse and waltzed out the door.

Kathleen was tempted to scream but that wouldn't achieve anything. She bit her lip. Why was Maura so horrid? When David, her fiancé, had been alive she'd been nicer. Not as nice as Bridget, but easier to live with.

Now Maura refused to spend any time with her. She went out every evening saying she had to be somewhere. She didn't elaborate, and Kathleen didn't press her. Maura was an adult and if she wanted to follow another path it wasn't up to Kathleen to stop her, no matter how much she disapproved. Maura had become very friendly with one of the women, Patricia, who worked in the sewing section of the sanctuary. Kathleen, who liked most everyone, didn't like Patricia, not least as she took her temper out on Bella and the other girls. Bella was outspoken and difficult sometimes to warm too, but the girl had a kind heart. She didn't say anything hurtful about anyone and wasn't a gossip, unlike Patricia. That woman seemed to delight in telling the group of women stories of orphans being sent on trains to become slaves to their new owners. Kathleen had challenged her more than once, but Patricia insisted she was just repeating what she read in the newspapers. Kathleen wished Bridget were here. Her sister was strong enough to put anyone, including Patricia Martin, back in her place.

Kathleen didn't believe her stories. She couldn't afford to. She was worried enough about her siblings. Not Liam and Annie, who wrote regularly about their new home with Carolyn and Geoff Rees in Riverside Springs. They were happy. But she hadn't heard anything from her brothers, Shane and Michael.

No one had. Lily had tried to find out more about where they had been placed but she could only find information which suggested they were on route to Cedar Falls, Iowa.

CHAPTER 3

NEW YORK

*I*t was chilly the next evening despite it being the end of April. Kathleen wrapped her shawl tighter around her shoulders, wishing she had thought to bring her coat. A cab trundled by, hitting a puddle in the process, and sending a shower of water over their small group. If it hadn't been for Mike's quick reflexes pulling Kathleen out of the way, she would have been soaked. She thanked the gentle giant with a warm smile which made him blush.

They could smell the tenement before they

reached it. The stench of boiling cabbage, un-washed bodies, and decades of discarded filth fought for dominance. Bella's face was a picture.

"I forget you never lived in the tenements, did you?" Kathleen asked her friend.

Holding her nose in a most unladylike way, Bella shook her head as if afraid to breathe in the air.

Kathleen's stomach roiled too but she fought hard to keep a smile on her face. She didn't want to offend her old neighbors; her friends who still lived in this vile place. Mrs. Fleming wasn't standing at her door to greet them as she usually did. A feeling of dread made the hairs on the back of her neck stand up. She moved closer to the door, but Lily laid a hand on her arm.

"Maybe we are too early?" Lily asked.

"Lily, you and I both know Mrs. Fleming is always ready an hour before we're due to ar-rive. Something is wrong."

"Wait here and I will check," Lily said.

"Not on your life. You need to watch out for yourself. You have someone else to think of now," Kathleen said gently, her eyes glancing to Lily's softly rounded stomach barely visible under her open coat. "Bella, please stay with Lily. I will come back as soon as I can."

Kathleen didn't wait for her friends to argue back. Her eyes met those of Mike's and he nodded slightly. He would stay with the ladies outside. Tommy followed Kathleen and she didn't argue; she was glad of his support.

She made her way deeper into the rooms, her heart beating so loudly, she thought it would wake the dead. What was wrong?

"Mrs. Fleming. It's Kathleen Collins. I came to…."

Kathleen came to a standstill as the vision before her started to make sense. The Fleming family were gathered around the double bed which had been dragged from its normal place against the wall to the center of the room nearer to the wood burning stove. The room, normally so clean and tidy, was in disarray.

The chairs were placed around the bed. Mrs. Fleming, pale and shrunken to a shadow of her former self, lay surrounded by her children.

"Ma, it's Kathleen Collins. Remember her? She used to live next door," Colm Fleming said gently, bending down nearer his mother's ear.

Kathleen caught Mr. Fleming's eye, his expression making the tears threaten to flow. She bent down beside the bed.

"Mrs. Fleming, it's Kathleen Collins. Why didn't you send someone for me?" Kathleen asked, forgetting Lily had been sent for last week.

"Ma said she wasn't sick enough. She seemed to be doing better than last week, but then yesterday she took a really bad turn. The doctor had to come," Jess said, her face white with shock and grief. Kathleen gave the ten-year old a quick hug.

Kathleen knew that families in these tenements didn't send for the doctor unless it was really serious. They couldn't afford his fees.

"What did he say?" she asked.

"He said there was nothing to be done. She will be gone by nightfall," Jess repeated tonelessly.

Kathleen gaped at the child who didn't appear to understand the harsh reality of the words she was repeating. Her eyes rose to meet those of Mr. Fleming and she saw he agreed with the doctor's assessment.

"Children, leave me be. I want to talk to Kathleen. Alone." Mrs. Fleming took an age to get the one sentence out, punctuating each word with a cough. "You too, Dave."

Kathleen waited for Dave Fleming to escort his children outside. Then she moved closer to her friend, taking Mrs. Fleming's hand in hers.

Mrs. Fleming tried to take her hand back. "You shouldn't touch me, love, don't know if it's catching." Mrs. Fleming coughed into a rag. Kathleen spotted the fresh blood. Still, she moved closer to the woman who had stood by her family when they needed help. She held Mrs. Fleming's hand tighter, wanting to erase the fear from her eyes.

"What can I do for you?" Kathleen asked. "Why didn't you send for me?"

"I thought I had more time. I didn't think it would take me so fast. My mam and gran had it, but with them it took years. Kathleen. My children. Will you make sure they are looked after? Dave will be able to cope with the elder boys, but he won't know how to deal with the young 'uns. The girls, they need a ma. They need…."

"Shush now, the girls will be just fine as will the rest of the family. We will look after them. Would you like some water?"

Kathleen held Mrs. Fleming up so she could take a small sip of water. She couldn't believe how light the woman was. She had faded away to almost nothing. Why hadn't she come to see the Flemings a couple of weeks ago? She might have been able to do something for them.

"Kathleen, can you ask…." The woman struggled to get the words out. It took every ounce of her strength to speak.

"What is it?"

"Ask Father Nelson to bury me in a decent grave. I have the money put by. I couldn't care less where they put me but, Dave, he will insist on it. Don't let him waste money though. I don't need the best casket or any of the trimmings. Heaven don't care about those things, but my family does."

Kathleen swallowed hard, the woman was being so brave. She nodded her head, not trusting herself to speak.

"I think you best send them back in, dear. Thank you."

"Oh, Mrs. Fleming, after everything you did for my family, I wish there was something I could do for you," Kathleen whispered, her voice shaking with the effort to stop her tears.

"There is. My girls."

Kathleen shouted for Dave to come back, not wanting the woman to die without her family by her side. She pulled out of the way and left the little family to it. She had to go and tell Lily and Bella.

CHAPTER 4

NEW YORK

*C*areful not to touch Lily for fear of carrying germs, she outlined what was happening. Lily paled, her hands going to her mouth.

"Mrs. Fleming? Why didn't she send us word when I didn't come last week? Why didn't she send for me again? Tell me it was urgent."

"She said she thought she had more time. She is worried about her family. I said we would look after them."

"Of course, we will. Dave Fleming is a

wonderful husband and father. He will be just fine with a little bit of help from us and his neighbors. I'm sure once people know they will help too."

Kathleen would have once agreed with Lily. When she lived here, neighbors tried to help each other. But times were even tougher now, there was less work and thus less money to go around. The people might have great intentions, but intentions couldn't make a dollar stretch further. When you were struggling to feed and keep a roof over your own family, charity wasn't something you could afford.

They didn't have to wait long. The wails of the children told them their friend had passed on.

"Tommy, take Lily home please," Kathleen said. "This is no place for her."

"What about you, Kathleen?" Lily asked, looking concerned.

"I am fine. I will stay with the Flemings. Tommy can escort you home, and Mini Mike can go for Father Nelson. You heard what the doctor said, Lily. You need to be especially careful."

"I will stay too. There might be something I can do," Bella said quickly. Kathleen gave her a grateful look before turning back to Lily.

Kathleen could see Lily was fighting the will to protect her child with her need to be there for their friend. "Mrs. Fleming wouldn't want you to risk the babe. Go. I will be fine. I'll be back tomorrow."

Kathleen took the basket of things from Mini Mike and turned to go back into the Flemings'. She took a second to say a quiet prayer for the woman who had done her best to shelter and protect the Collins family when they needed her. It was time for her to repay the favor by making sure her young ones were looked after.

Twin girls looked up as Kathleen and Bella made their way inside. She hadn't noticed them before. Given their age, she assumed they were friends of Helen Fleming, Mrs. Fleming's youngest daughter. The twins were visibly upset.

Kathleen bent down to greet them. "Girls, maybe you should go home. Mrs. Fleming has died and her family need time to say goodbye."

"We don't got a home," one of the girls said. "Not anymore. We were staying here."

Kathleen looked into the girl's eyes and saw she was telling the truth. The poor child looked scared to bits, but she was trying to be brave, holding her sister's hand tight.

"I'm sorry, I didn't know that. My name is Kathleen Collins. Mrs. Fleming once looked after my family too."

"She was a really nice lady. Da said she would look after us. What's going to happen now?"

Kathleen didn't know. She doubted Dave Fleming would be able to mind his own brood, without worrying about extras.

"I will check with Mr. Fleming. But for now, why don't you sit down and have a cookie. They were baked today and are delicious."

The girls rubbed their hands on their dresses before taking the cookies.

"You go into your friends. I will stay with these girls," Bella said. "I don't want to go inside as I don't know the family."

"Thanks, Bella," Kathleen whispered before she hurried into the room where the family sat around the bed. Mrs. Fleming would need to be laid out. She caught Colm Fleming's eye and motioned the lad over to her. They were of a similar age.

"Colm, I am so sorry for your loss. Your ma was a good woman."

"Thanks, Kathleen. I wish I'd known how bad she was, but she hid it."

"Mothers are like that," Kathleen added softly, thinking of her own mam. "Colm, there are twin girls outside. They said they live here."

"Aye, Megan and Eileen, Tom Doyle's six-year-old young 'uns. Tom went blind in an accident down the mill years back. His missus left about a year after and took the baby with her. Nobody knows where she went. Ma took the twins in as Tom couldn't handle them anymore. He said he would come back with some money, but he never showed up."

"So, they've been abandoned?"

Colm looked around to check no one was listening.

"Don't tell the Priest, but rumor has it Mrs. Doyle done away with herself. Ma said Tom was sick with grief. Said the girls would be better off here, but now…Da won't be able to mind them too. You will have to take them."

"Me?"

"To Lily Doherty. Your Bridget took a train load of orphans away last year. The Doyle girls need a home."

Kathleen thought of the two little ones outside and her heart melted. Six years old and all they had was each other.

"Sorry, Kathleen, but what else can we do?" Colm asked. "I can't mind them. I got a job on the railways. I was lucky after all the closures 'cause of the crash in shares. Da has his hands full here."

"I know, Colm. Best of luck with the job. I will stay here, but Bella, my friend, will take the twins to Lily."

"I miss you, Kathleen." His cheeks flushed as it hit him what he had said. "I mean, I miss all of you, Shane most of all. Tell him I said hello when you next hear from him."

Kathleen found herself nodding. Colm gave her hand a gentle squeeze before taking his place back with his family. They were saying the prayers for the dead.

CHAPTER 5

NEW YORK

"*M*iss, what's going to happen to us?"

Bella looked down at the little girl, her arm wrapped around her sister, both faces smeared with cookies.

"I don't know, Megan, isn't it?" she asked the one who had spoken.

The girl nodded.

"My friend Kathleen will be back in a minute."

To her relief, Kathleen didn't take long inside the small room. "Bella, can you take the twins back to the sanctuary. I need to stay here and help the family. I might be all night."

"Are you sure I can't do anything to help you?" Bella asked, despite not wanting to go inside. Dead bodies scared her.

"Thank you, but no. You take the girls, that's helping me. I will see you later."

The twins looked between Bella and Kathleen.

"We don't want to leave. We want to stay here, our da knows we are here. He said he'd come back."

Bella exchanged a quick look with Kathleen before kneeling, so she would be on the same level as Megan.

"Megan, we can't stay here as lots of people will come to say goodbye to Mrs. Fleming. I am going to take you to where we live and give you some dinner. You can stay with us for a few nights, and if your da comes, someone will tell him where you are."

"I'll tell him, Megan. You go on with these nice ladies. That's what Mam would have wanted you to do," a red-haired lad with freckles said.

"Thanks, Colm," Kathleen answered. "Can you go for the midwife for me please. Someone needs to see to your mam."

The young man was gone before Bella could offer her condolences.

"That was Colm Fleming, he and my brother Shane were once best friends," Kathleen explained before turning to go back into the room.

Bella took the girls' hands and walked them slowly back to the sanctuary. Tommy came with them despite her protests.

"Ain't safe for you to be walking the streets, Miss Bella. That's for sure," he mumbled. She didn't argue with him but insisted he go back to wait for Kathleen once he had something to eat. She didn't want anything to happen to her friend.

The twins didn't seem hungry, so she took them upstairs where she gave them a bath and put them to bed. They wanted to share a bed, so she decided to give them the bed in her room. Eileen cried but Megan didn't shed a tear which worried Bella. She wondered how the twins had ended up with Mrs. Fleming.

"Please don't leave us. We don't like the dark," Megan said quietly.

"I won't leave you. I will sleep here on the floor," she promised. She told them a story until they fell asleep. She watched the two little innocent faces and wondered what life had in store for them now.

THANKFUL BELLA HAD TAKEN the twins, Kathleen waited for the midwife. The same woman did the birthing and laying out of the dead. But Colm sent word to say she was at a birth so wouldn't be able to come till morning. Annoyed Colm didn't make an appearance, Kathleen wasn't sure what to do. She couldn't leave Mrs. Fleming; even in death the woman deserved her dignity. She would have been the first to ensure a body was decent when the priest arrived. So, Kathleen boiled some water on the stove, then asked Dave Fleming to leave. They left Jess, Mrs. Fleming's ten-year-old, with Kathleen.

Together they washed the woman down and changed her into a clean shift. They couldn't do anything about the bed, it being the only one in the house.

Father Nelson arrived soon after. Before he got a chance to walk inside to Mrs. Fleming, Kathleen explained she had asked Bella to take the Doyle girls to the sanctuary.

"Good idea, Kathleen, we will deal with them tomorrow. I can't believe she's gone. She was a wonderful woman."

Father Nelson smiled at her, but Kathleen could see the older man was deeply affected by the death of Mrs. Fleming. The warm-hearted woman had been the soul of this community.

CHAPTER 6

NEW YORK

*B*ella went looking for Kathleen the next morning having asked Cook to look after the Doyle girls. She left the twins tucking into big bowls of creamy porridge with added cream and sugar. Cook had taken one look at the little ones and decided they needed fattening up.

She found Kathleen in the sewing room.

"I thought you would be with the Flemings. Don't you have to go to the funeral?" Bella asked, wanting to hug Kathleen but she didn't feel able. She was getting better at showing her feelings, but this didn't extend to physical displays of affection.

"It's tomorrow morning. Mrs. Fleming has a sister who is coming, and Dave's brother will be back from his trip too. They thought it best to wait," Kathleen replied, the red circles around her eyes showing she had been crying. She looked shattered.

"Why don't you go back to bed? I can do your quota," Bella offered.

"You have your own work to do but thank you. I will be fine. Losing Mrs. Fleming, it got me thinking about my own family. Mam and Da."

Bella wasn't sure how to respond. She had never known her da and she only had a vague memory of a mother figure. She picked up her work and went to sit at her machine. Then she remembered the twins.

"What should I do with the girls? I let them sleep in my room last night. Cook is with them now."

Kathleen looked unsure. "I guess we should ask Mrs. Wilson or Lily."

"Lily won't be here today according to Cook. Mrs. Wilson will be in later," Bella volunteered before threading the needle for her machine. "I could bring in a blanket and some toys left over from the last group of kids. They could play over there. I don't think the other ladies will mind. Especially under the circumstances. They are bound to know Mrs. Fleming."

"Good idea. I will go fetch them," Kathleen suggested.

Bella was glad Kathleen went to get the girls. Although she felt sorry for them and didn't regret letting them share her bed, she didn't want to get too close to them. Children didn't last long in the sanctuary. They either went back to their parents or they joined orphan trains and were sent west. She didn't want to risk getting hurt. But the twins called to her. She felt for them in a way she hadn't allowed herself to feel for Jacob, Lizzie, or any of the other children who had lived at the sanctuary since she'd arrived.

She had to be careful. The twins were so sweet and lovable she could already tell giving them up to their new home would be difficult. And that was only after one day. Disgusted at her weakness, she put her head down and got to work.

Sometime later, Kathleen returned with the girls who played on the blanket while the women worked. The atmosphere in the room was strained as Bella had expected it to be. Most of the women knew Mrs. Fleming personally or by reputation. Her loss would leave its mark. Bella couldn't help thinking how different it would be if she were to die. Who would mourn her? Kathleen would, maybe even Lily as they had grown closer over the last few months. Bridget, Kathleen's sister had advised Bella to trust Lily and she'd been right. But still only two people in the whole world would mourn at her funeral. Some legacy she would leave.

"What has you looking so glum, Bella?" Kathleen asked, her face a mask of concern. "You didn't know Mrs. Fleming. Has her death reminded you of someone special?"

"No, not really. I was just thinking about who would be at my funeral if I were to die."

Kathleen paled in front of her. She didn't get a chance to apologize as her friend admonished her.

"Mary Mother of Jesus, why would you be thinking something like that now? You are young and healthy. Nothing is going to happen to you, Bella. I won't let it."

CHAPTER 7

NEW YORK

athleen looked around the church, packed to the rafters for the funeral service, and afterwards the large procession followed the coffin to the grave-yard. Closing her eyes, she could picture the smile on her neighbor's face knowing all these people turned out to pay their respects. She wouldn't have believed she was so highly thought of. That was what made Mrs. Fleming special. She did everything for others because it was the right thing to do, not because of how it made her look.

Mrs. Fleming was laid to rest surrounded by her family, neighbors, and the families of all those she had helped over the years. There were so many people who came up to Dave Fleming afterward to pass on their condolences and tell him how his wife had helped them.

"I knew Darlene was special, but I had no idea she helped so many. She had a heart the size of Texas," Mr. Fleming told Kathleen. "That was where she was from, you know. Her pa settled there after the war. I should have stayed in Texas, but they said there were more opportunities in New York. But that was a lie. Never could give her the life she deserved, and now she's gone."

"She loved you and her family, Mr. Fleming. I never saw her without a big smile on her face. She was happy."

"Kathleen is right, Mr. Fleming. Your wife told me how proud she was of you and her family," Lily said firmly. "You worked hard to support them and didn't drink your wages every night. She was always telling us how good you were. She was proud to be your wife."

The man looked to Lily, his cheeks crimson at her praise. "I was the one who was proud."

He walked away, his hat held in his hands, his shoulders slumped in defeat. Kathleen caught one of the younger Fleming girls going after him.

"Leave your pa alone for a bit, Helen. He needs some time to himself," she told the girl gently.

"Why did God have to do this to us? We needed our ma. He has plenty of people in heaven. Why did he have to take her too?" Helen asked, standing close to Kathleen.

"I don't know the answer to that, love." Kathleen put her arm around the little girl, wishing she could find words of comfort, but nothing was going to help the eight-year-old girl. With time she would learn to deal with the pain of losing her ma, but she would never get over it. Kathleen knew that from personal experience.

She was glad the Doyle girls weren't at the church. Bella was looking after them back in the sanctuary. Lily had decided a funeral was no place for the twins, especially as nobody knew where their da was. Dave Fleming had confirmed what Colm had told her, adding the fact that Mr. Doyle was unlikely to return. She looked around her again, taking everything in so she could tell Bridget all about it in her letter. Bridget would be devastated to hear about Mrs. Fleming dying, but at least Kathleen could tell her how much the community showed their respect.

As she gazed around the church, she spied many from the local gangs. She was surprised to find them here in the church, yet she knew Mrs. Fleming had held their respect. The woman had refused to put up with any of their nonsense as she called it, she had never shown any fear of even the worst of the gang leaders.

If anything, she treated them like badly be-haved children. It had worked too. There had been no instances of gang violence breaking out in Mrs. Fleming's tenement. Kathleen hoped that wouldn't change now.

CHAPTER 8

CHEYENNE, WYOMING

"Good morning, Bridget. Carl said you were feeling a bit brighter this morning," Edwina Powell said, her eyes full of concern.

"Thank you, Edwina. The traveling caught up with me. How is Sally this morning?"

"She is bored already. Anthony told her she has to rest her leg. The plaster will come off next week," Edwina said, glancing toward her daughter's temporary bedroom. The Powells had converted a room on the ground floor to save Sally having to climb the stairs.

"It is so good of you to invite us to stay with you while we were visiting Cheyenne. Sally is a changed girl from the one we left with you last year."

"She is happier, isn't she? The operations have taken their toll, but Anthony is confident she will walk without pain after this last one."

Happier was an understatement. If only all the orphans the Outplacement Society placed were as lucky as young Sally. The child had been left with an untreated broken leg after an accident years previously. The Powell's had not only adopted her, but Anthony had used his medical ability to fix her leg. It had taken three operations, but everyone was hopeful the last one had been successful.

The door opened as her husband Carl came in, a look of concern on his face. "Morning, darling. I went to send a telegram and picked one up for you."

Bridget's hand shook as she took the telegram from him.

"I will go put the kettle on," Edwina said

softly. "Come into the kitchen when you are ready."

Bridget looked at her friend gratefully. If it was bad news, she wanted to be alone with her husband. She opened the telegram and quickly scanned the contents.

"Bad news?" Carl asked, putting his arm around her shoulder.

Bridget nodded, swallowing to get rid of the lump in her throat. "Kathleen wrote to tell me our old neighbor has died. Mrs. Fleming. She was so good to us when Mam was ill. She was the lady who told the people who were looking for me we had moved to our cousin's place."

Carl pulled her close and cuddled her. "I'm sorry about your friend."

"I wonder what will happen to her family, not to mention those she helped in that horrible tenement. She will be sorely missed by many." Bridget knew nobody would ever be able to quantify how many people relied on Mrs. Fleming. Her friend had helped Lily distribute food and clothing to those who were too proud to admit they needed help.

"I will take you to see Mr. Fleming when we get back to New York," Carl said before giving her a hug.

Bridget lay her head on his shoulder, thankful she had him by her side. She was nervous about returning to New York. It had been some time since she had injured Mr. Oak Jr. when she ran from his unwanted attentions, but had it been long enough?

"Let's go and put Edwina out of her misery. She is bound to be concerned," Carl murmured, kissing the top of her head.

She loved her husband so much. He was always thinking of others. She followed him into the kitchen where Edwina was setting plates on the table.

"Bridget got some bad news from home. A friend of hers passed away," Carl said as he took a seat.

"Mrs. Fleming. She was a neighbor and a young mother to five children," Bridget explained. "We lived beside them when my own parents were alive."

"I am sorry for your loss. Will you return to New York sooner than planned now?" Edwina asked as she poured tea into Bridget's cup. It was another example of her kindness. She had bought tea specially for their visit as she and her husband were coffee drinkers.

Bridget exchanged a look with Carl. There was no point in returning now, the funeral would be over and there was still work to be done here in Cheyenne.

"No, Edwina. We still have work to do here, following up some of the placements. Mrs. Fleming would understand the children come first," Carl confirmed, his eyes searching Bridget's.

A wave of love passed through her. She knew her husband would take her back to New York today if she said she wanted to go.

"She sounds like a wonderful woman. Would you like me to cancel the coffee morning? We could postpone it to next week?" Edwina asked.

Bridget wanted to say yes but that was being selfish. Edwina had put a lot of work into organizing a group of people to come to her home for a chat about the Outplacement Society. In addition to prospective parents, Edwina had also invited those with positions of responsibility in Cheyenne. The mayor, the teacher, a pastor, and some other leading lights of the community would be useful in finding new homes and opportunities for the children from New York.

"No, thank you, Edwina, but you are kind to offer. I know how much work you have put into making this morning a success. Carl and I have come up with a series of suggestions on how to make the orphan trains more effective. We are looking forward to discussing them with your friends and listening to their views and opinions. When we get back to New York, we will sit down with Father Nelson and the other representatives of the Outplacement Society. I look forward to telling them about your achievements."

Edwina blushed a becoming shade of pink. "I think you overstate what I did. It didn't take much to speak to a few people."

"If you hadn't adopted Sally in the first place, those people wouldn't be listening in quite the same way," Bridget replied firmly.

"I love Sally like she was my own. In fact, Anthony and I would be open to offering another child a home. When you spoke about the attitudes some people have, you know how some believe that as long as the children were taken off the streets of New York and sent somewhere—anywhere—else, it was a blessing, we felt we needed to do more."

"Oh, Edwina, that's wonderful. It's true that for some people the interests of the children couldn't be further from their minds, but thankfully we have met people like yourself and Anthony. Those willing to open their hearts to the children. Finding homes like yours makes it all worthwhile."

Bridget and Carl were determined to protect the children from being exploited in any way they could.

"We won't be staying in New York long. I telegraphed Father Nelson to tell him we were staying in Cheyenne for a couple of weeks and he wrote back to me. I collected his letter first thing this morning."

"What does he say?" Bridget asked.

Carl read out a few pages to her. The Priest was looking forward to their return but also worried about the Oaks. He also wrote of a group of orphans that needed to be escorted to towns along the same route they had taken before. Bridget couldn't help but wonder if Father Nelson had deliberately put the trip together, so they got a chance to visit Liam and Annie. It would be wonderful to see her younger siblings again. She missed them, but knew they were enjoying a happy and stable life with their new adoptive parents.

So far, all the placements made on her first orphan trip had worked out well. In addition to

Sally, they had visited most of the other children too. Some were working as indentured servants. They worked long hours but were treated fairly. Others enjoyed a closer bond with the families who had accepted them. Like Sally, some of the other children had been formally adopted. She had been thrilled to catch up with the Kelly siblings. Jacob Kelly was like a new person, he walked straighter and was doing well at school. This time last year he hadn't been able to read and now he read the newspaper with his father every evening. His sister Lizzie—Elizabeth, she corrected herself quickly—was just as exquisite-looking as she had always been. Dressed now in luxury clothes and looking every inch the precious daughter of a well-to-do couple, Bridget had been thrilled to see she hadn't lost her kind heart. The newly formed family was devoted to each other. She glanced up and caught Edwina's eye.

"Are you nervous about this morning, Edwina?"

"No, Bridget, not really. All I have to do is tell them about Sally, and I could talk about my daughter until the cows came home."

Bridget loved the look of love on the older woman's face. Some days her work brought nothing but joy. She closed her eyes and said a quick prayer for Darlene Fleming. She hoped she was resting in the arms of the Lord and promised to do anything she could to help her family.

CHAPTER 9

NEW YORK

*B*ella looked up from her machine as Mrs. Wilson came into the room. She was working extra time on her own designs. Lily had agreed to her and Kathleen using the machines for their own projects. She hoped to sell the dresses she was working on to a local market stall holder.

"Bella, can you look after the Doyle twins today," Mrs. Wilson asked. "I have errands to run and, well, there is nobody else."

Bella sighed, wanting to refuse. But Mrs. Wilson had been good to her. Also, she knew the supervisor was fair and would have asked the others. The fact she was asking Bella again meant Maura, Patricia, and the other women had refused. Kathleen would usually step in, but she had gone to see the Fleming family. Dave was struggling to cope with the girls, and Kathleen had volunteered to teach young Jess and Helen how to keep house. Lily and everyone at the sanctuary didn't want the family to be split up.

"They will have to be quiet. I have a lot of work to do," Bella responded. She didn't like getting close to the children who came to the sanctuary as they always left. She hated goodbyes.

Megan and Eileen started off well-behaved, sitting in the corner of the sewing room playing quietly. But then they got bored.

"Bella, will you play with us?" Megan asked.

"Not now, Megan. I have work to do."

"But can't you do it later? Please, Bella, we want to play. Pa always had time for us. Mrs.

Fleming did, too," Megan pleaded, her angelic smile lighting up her face. The girls weren't what you would call beautiful, they had bright red hair, freckles, and crooked teeth. But when Megan smiled like that, few could resist. Eileen was the quieter twin, but she was a charmer too with her blue eyes and bright smile.

"All right. What do you want to play?" Bella asked, giving in to their hopeful smiles.

"Do you know any games?" Megan asked.

Bella didn't.

"Why? What did you play when you were young?" Megan asked, her head cocked to one side as she studied Bella.

She wasn't about to tell Megan what her childhood had been like. That would give the twins nightmares.

"I can't remember, Megan. Why don't you show me a game you enjoy playing? Maybe a song? Or would you like to make a rag doll?"

"Make a doll? Can we really do that?"

Megan asked excitedly. Then her face fell. "But we can't sew."

Eileen sat sucking her thumb, but her eyes flew between Megan and Bella showing she was listening to every word. Bella wondered if she ever did anything she wanted or was she content for Megan to always lead.

"I can teach you. See that basket over there? That's where we keep spare bits of material. We usually make them into quilts, but nobody will mind us taking some for a doll." Bella hoped that was true.

"Two dolls. We need one each," Eileen insisted.

Bella smiled. So that was how it was. For a child who didn't say much, Eileen knew what she wanted.

Surprised, she found she enjoyed the time with the girls. Mrs. Wilson arrived back all too soon.

"Look, Mrs. Wilson, Bella is helping us make dolls," Megan said as the supervisor came in.

Mrs. Wilson raised her eyebrows, making Bella worry that she'd done something wrong.

"It's only from remnants. I didn't use any of the fabric we need. I had to do something to keep them busy," Bella tried to explain.

Mrs. Wilson looked annoyed. "Enough Bella. There is no need to get so defensive. I was going to praise you for your initiative."

"Oh," Bella said, feeling ashamed. "Sorry."

The supervisor just tutted before saying, "Come on, girls, let's go. Bella has work to do."

"Can we come back tomorrow? Will you help us finish the dolls? Please?" Megan asked.

Bella looked at Mrs. Wilson who didn't say a word.

"You can, but only if you do everything Mrs. Wilson tells you to do."

"Thank you, Bella." Megan threw her arms around Bella and hugged her. Eileen joined in. Bella didn't have time to react as the girls raced off.

"Children are good judges of character,

Bella," Mrs. Wilson said as she followed the girls out of the room. The twins had liked her and wanted to spend more time with her. It was a nice feeling. She had to stay behind to catch up with her work for the day, but she didn't mind. She was looking forward to spending more time with the girls tomorrow.

CHAPTER 10

NEW YORK

Kathleen was humming as Bella approached her. Kathleen stopped sewing to look at the bundle of shirts in Bella's arms.

"Was he happy with the last lot of work we did?" Kathleen asked, taking some of the shirts.

"Yes, so happy he increased the order. It was a fantastic idea to ask him to work with us direct rather than going through the agent." Bella had believed Kathleen was out of her mind when she'd first come up with the idea of approaching Mr. Herschel, a tailor with a local workshop and a store on Fifth Avenue, with a business idea.

By asking Mr. Herschel to deal with the sanctuary direct rather than using a middleman, they were able to give Mr. Herschel a more favorable price while earning more money per shirt. This helped Lily keep the sanctuary open to provide for those who needed it.

"He is so happy, he said he is going to recommend some of his friends use us as well," Bella said happily.

"Oh, that is good news. Lily might look less worried," Kathleen responded.

"She said some of Mr. Prentice's richest friends had lost a lot of money in business and some were facing ruin. She also said that was why more people were out of work."

"Yet Mr. Hershel and his fine goods store seems to be expanding. It's funny how some people survive and prosper no matter what happens, isn't it?" Kathleen asked.

"I am glad they do because if Mr. Hershel

keeps increasing his orders, we will have lots of money," Bella said. She firmly believed money was the answer to a lot of problems. The rich never had to worry about where they would sleep or what they would eat. She was determined never to be poor again, no matter how hard she had to work. Kathleen was humming again.

"Why do you hum that same tune?" Bella asked.

"Mam used to sing it when I was younger. I guess it's a habit," Kathleen replied.

"You are so lucky to remember your mam. I don't remember anything about mine." That wasn't strictly true. She remembered a smell of rosewater and a necklace she'd liked to play with. When she tried hard to remember, she could see a shape but never a face. "She dumped me at the foundling hospital when I was around two years old. I have no idea why she kept me so long then had to dump me. My adopted mother said it was because I was a bas—"

"Don't, Bella, that horrible word should never be used by anyone. Maybe your dad died, and your ma couldn't afford to keep you. I am sure she would have preferred to keep you with her."

Bella knew her friend loved her, but did she really mean what she said?

"Do you really think so?" Bella asked.

"Yes, I do," Kathleen replied firmly. She didn't know what Bella's mother had been thinking, but why not give her some comfort. They were of a similar age, yet Bella had lived a lifetime experience-wise. She had been sent from New York on an orphan train when she was little and had been treated badly. The scars on her back were horrible, but the non-visible scars were probably worse. Bella didn't trust anyone. Or at least she hadn't until she'd met Bridget who had struck up a rapport with her. When Bridget left, Bella and Kathleen had become close.

"Kathleen, will you leave when Bridget comes back?"

Kathleen put her sewing to one side, facing Bella with complete concentration. "Bridget wants me to go to Riverside Springs. Why don't you come too?"

"Leave the sanctuary?" Bella asked, sounding surprised. "No, I couldn't do that."

"Yes, you could," Kathleen reassured her. "You'll have to one day. You know Lily would love to provide you with a home forever, but that's not possible. There isn't enough money even with the deal we did with Mr. Hershel."

"I can't go on an orphan train again, Kathleen."

The whispered words screamed pain. Kathleen prayed for the right words to reassure her friend.

"It won't be like your first experience. First, you wouldn't be alone, and you're not six years old. We are old enough to get married and have our own families."

"That's all right for you. But nobody out there will want me," Bella said.

Kathleen wished she could wipe the fear

and mistrust from Bella's eyes, but her friend had been kicked so often, she just couldn't expect people not to be mean.

"That's not true. You are very pretty and when you let people get to know you, you have a lovely heart. You just pretend to be horrible, so people can't hurt you," Kathleen said.

"Ha! Most of the women here wouldn't agree with you. Patricia says—"

"I don't care what Patricia says," Kathleen interrupted. "Or anyone else for that matter. I know you. The real you."

Bella didn't respond. She picked up her sewing and started working at it again.

Kathleen took her lead and set about threading the machine once more.

"Kathleen?"

"Yeah." Kathleen tried to speak with the thread in her mouth.

Bella stopped working to look at her.

"Do you really think I could find a nice man and have a family?"

Kathleen nodded as she tried to untangle

the threads blocking the machine. She stopped as Maura and Patricia walked into the sewing room, wincing at the malicious expression on Patricia's face.

"Ha, you have as much chance of finding a decent man as I have of winning the hand of the Prince of England. Did you hear that, Maura? Our Bella thinks she can marry a fine man and your sister is egging her on."

Kathleen looked to Maura, waiting for her older sister to tell Patricia to shut up, but she said nothing. Instead, she looked at Bella as if she was something nasty she had walked on. Kathleen felt her temper rising. Something that seemed to happen with increasing regularity around Maura.

"Patricia Martin, if you can't say anything nice, just stay quiet will you," Kathleen retorted, raising her voice.

Patricia opened her mouth to respond but Lily got there first.

"Ladies, please."

The women jumped, not having seen Lily walk into the room.

"Patricia, I have already spoken to you about being kind to others. One of the rules of the sanctuary is to treat everyone with respect. You should apologize to Bella."

Lily looked at Patricia who simply stared back at her. Kathleen's gaze flickered from one to the other, wondering who would give in first. After a few tense seconds, Patricia flung a halfhearted apology in Bella's direction.

"I apologize for shouting," Kathleen added, eager to smooth things over. She didn't want Lily to be upset, not in her condition.

Lily smiled but it didn't reach her eyes. She cast a worried look at Patricia and Maura before turning her attention back to Kathleen.

"Bridget and Carl are due on the one o'clock train. I came in to see if you would like to meet them at the station or wait for them to call here. They'll be staying at my house while they are in New York, since it wouldn't be suitable for Carl to reside at the sanctuary."

Kathleen felt like a child at Christmas. She would have probably jumped up and down if it had only been herself and Lily in the room. Instead, she restrained herself.

"I would love to meet them at the station. Are you coming, Maura?" Kathleen asked, her excitement making her forget about her sister's unkindness.

"No. I have work to do." Maura's tone suggested she couldn't be less interested in seeing Bridget. Tempted to rebuke her, Kathleen decided to stay quiet. Her reunion with Bridget would be better if Maura wasn't there to ruin things.

"Mike will collect you at noon, Kathleen. Good day, ladies."

Lily swept out of the room but not before Kathleen saw her expression. She didn't appear to be angry as Kathleen expected, given Maura's attitude. But she looked incredibly sad.

CHAPTER 11

NEW YORK

athleen stood at the railing waiting for the passengers to disembark. As soon as she saw Bridget, she picked up her skirts and flew across the platform. It wasn't ladylike, but she didn't care.

"Bridget, oh how I have missed you," she said, throwing herself into Bridget's arms.

Her sister hugged her close. Then, smiling at her, she turned to the man at her side and said. "This is Kathleen, my younger sister. Kathleen, you remember Carl?"

Suddenly feeling shy, Kathleen doubted the

man would remember her from their brief meeting at the sanctuary when he had come to talk to Lizzie and Jacob about traveling on the orphan train and what it involved.

"Nice to meet you again, Kathleen. I have heard so much about you from Liam and Annie. And Bridget, of course."

"Nice to meet you too. How are the children? They sound so happy in their letters."

Bridget took Kathleen's arm, leaving her husband to take care of their bags. "Happy? I think that is an understatement. You should see the house they live in. Their new parents, Geoff Rees and his wife, Carolyn, are wonderful. You will get to meet them when you come to Riverside Springs." Bridget looked around her. "I can't believe I forgot how busy this station gets. Thank you for coming to collect us. Where is Lily?"

"Waiting impatiently in the buggy. She wanted to come to the platform, but we decided it was better for her to wait."

"We?" Bridget asked.

Kathleen laughed. "I suggested it would be better and Mini Mike agreed. He's taking his promise to Charlie very seriously. But with Charlie away in Washington, who else will stop Lily from overdoing things? The doctor says she must be careful."

Bridget hugged her close again making Kathleen glad her sister was here, she'd missed her. Also, she might be able to do something about Maura. As if she read her mind, Bridget asked how their elder sister was.

"I missed you so much, Kathleen. Maura too. How is she?" Bridget asked.

Kathleen couldn't look at Bridget. She didn't feel right talking badly about Maura. But was it fair not to prepare Bridget for what lay ahead?

"Kathleen? Is she ill? What aren't you telling me?"

"She is fit and healthy," Kathleen said. "She just... well, you will see for yourself soon enough. Look, there's Lily. She'll jump out of that buggy if you don't get over to her quickly."

Bridget gave her a look which told her that the subject of Maura hadn't been abandoned.

"You go and speak to Lily. I'll wait here to make sure Carl finds us. Go on."

Bridget walked quickly over to see Lily. Kathleen watched her sister and friend greet each other like long-lost siblings. That was how it should be between Maura and Bridget, but that wasn't going to happen. She hoped Maura would at least keep a civil tongue in her head.

CHAPTER 12

NEW YORK

Kathleen looked up from the dinner table, smiling at the people around her. She couldn't remember the last time she was so happy. Bridget and Carl were a great match, and it was obvious to everyone they were happy together. They had shared news of Annie and Liam's new home. Riverside Springs sounded like an amazing place to live.

"That was a wonderful meal, thank you, Lily," Father Nelson said as he led their little group into Lily's sitting room.

"It was indeed, thank you, Mrs. Doherty, for looking after us so well and for inviting us to stay in your fine home."

"Carl, please don't call me Mrs. Doherty. That's the name of Charlie's mother. My name is Lily and I consider you one of the family now." Lily took a seat before she continued, "Don't thank me for dinner, Father. It was all Cook's doing. She is intent on feeding me up with Charlie being away. I will be the size of a house when he comes back."

"You will be big soon even if she doesn't feed you up. I am so happy about the baby, Lily. Have you thought about a name?" Bridget asked.

"A few. Charlie is quite sure he wants to call her Erin if she is a girl but as yet we haven't agreed on a boy's name."

Lily leaned back into her chair. The poor woman looked exhausted, as though pregnancy was draining her of all her strength. Kathleen hoped she was being as careful as the doctor had suggested.

"Where is Charlie?" Bridget asked. "Is he away with work?"

Kathleen was intrigued by the guilty expression on Lily's face. What was going on?

"I hoped he would be back before Bridget and Carl got back," Lily said, looking at Bridget and her husband before turning to glance at Kathleen. Then she continued, her gaze focused on Carl.

"Kathleen told me about how your baby sister disappeared after going on the Orphan Train years back, Carl. I discussed it with Charlie, who you might know works as an investigator for a law firm. Anyway, we thought he might be able to find her."

Carl moved forward in his chair, his hopeful expression making his face light up. Kathleen couldn't believe her ears, she hadn't expected Lily to do anything. But knowing the couple like she did, she should have known they would try to help.

"And?" Carl asked.

"I'm sorry, but as of yet, Charlie has been

unsuccessful. There have been a few leads but, given her age at the time and how long ago it was, well, I guess I shouldn't have said anything." Lily looked to be on the verge of tears.

"It was my fault. I encouraged Lily by telling her about Hope in the first place," Kathleen admitted quickly. "I thought it was such a sad story, and it would be lovely to have a happy ending."

Lily shook her head. "I take full responsibility. Kathleen didn't know Charlie had gone looking for Hope. She just told us about her."

Father Nelson intervened. "I am responsible too. I provided some leads for Charlie. I only wish I had been able to help more, but the record keeping back then wasn't always as good as it could be."

"Is there no chance of finding her?" Carl asked.

Kathleen noticed as Bridget took Carl's hand, giving him her support. They were a good couple, she decided.

Lily and Father Nelson exchanged a look

as they shifted in their seats. Kathleen saw both hoped to avoid that question.

"Father Nelson was told the records were closed and nobody could have access to them. We did some digging anyway and followed up on some leads, but nothing has come of them. But we will continue trying. Charlie has made some contacts in Illinois and they will continue the search," Lily explained. "I am so sorry. The last thing we wanted was to cause you more hurt."

"Illinois?" Carl repeated.

"Yes, it would seem that's where the orphan train carrying Hope was sent. But a lot of the families who adopted children, particularly the younger ones, changed their names."

"Yes, we know. It happened with one of the babies we brought with us. But they kept her real name as her second name," Bridget said, still holding Carl's hand.

"Thank you, Father Nelson, and you, Lily, for trying to help. I admit I have also tried to find Hope a few times but without success,"

Carl said, before adding, "Maybe it's just better for us to leave things as they are."

Kathleen couldn't agree. She knew if it were Liam or Annie who had gone missing, she would have searched the country. As it was, she was determined to find out where Shane and Michael were. She assumed Bridget felt the same but now was not the time to discuss their brothers.

Silence lingered so she decided to change the subject.

"I can't believe you enjoy working as an outplacement agent, Bridget. I mean, I know you enjoy helping others," Kathleen said. "But I thought you would find it too painful to leave the children behind."

Bridget exchanged a rueful look with her husband. She had written about some of their disagreements over how the children were handled, but Kathleen knew both had the best interests of their charges at heart.

"At times it is horrible. I find it hard saying goodbye to the children but…" Bridget took a breath, "Sometimes it is wonderful to place children in homes. For example, when Jacob was adopted, I cried with happiness."

"Jacob?" Kathleen queried. "You mean the boy who lived in the sanctuary for a while with his sister Lizzie?"

"Yes, that's the one. He gave up his chance for adoption in order for Lizzie to find a wonderful home. His actions made the people adopting his sister realize he was a special boy. So, they took him too. I cried with joy," Bridget said.

"She nearly drowned us all," Carl joked, looking at his wife with so much love in his expression.

Bridget returned Carl's gaze and he gave her a slight nod. "Carl and I have some ideas on how to make the orphan trains work better. We found quite a few of the representatives acting on behalf of the outplacement agency never checked up on the children. We want to make sure that every child is visited at least once a year, preferably more often."

"That is what was agreed," Father Nelson replied, his expression suggesting they were complicating matters.

"It was, but it isn't happening, at least not in every case," Bridget said softly. "But we hope we can change that. We can also change the process. At the moment, anyone who wants a child gets one."

"And the problem with that is?" The priest obviously didn't like the process being questioned. Kathleen remembered that the founder of their organization, Charles Brace, was known to Father Nelson. She hoped her sister and brother-in-law continued to be diplomatic, or it would turn into a very uncomfortable evening. She hated conflict.

Carl shifted in his seat, exchanging a look with Bridget before he answered the priest. "Father, rather than go into a delicate subject, let's just say that some of the homes were not the type to say prayers at bedtime."

Kathleen watched the priest turn red then go pale. She wasn't sure what type of home

Carl was talking about, but it was obvious it wasn't a good one. She sensed the discussion might be more open if she made herself scarce.

"I think it's time I went home. And Lily, you need to go to bed. You don't want to get overtired."

Lily looked like she was about to stamp her foot. "Oh, my word, I am not the first woman to ever have a baby. There is no reason to fuss so much."

"There is every reason, Lily. Kathleen is right." Bridget took her sister's hands and walked her to the door where Mini Mike waited to escort Kathleen back to the sanctuary.

"I take it Maura is not cooking up a feast in honor of my homecoming?" Bridget whispered as soon as they left the others behind them.

Her eyes searched Kathleen's face, making it difficult for her to tell Bridget anything but the truth.

"She missed you, you're her sister," Kathleen said, but her voice lacked conviction. She couldn't lie.

"If she missed me that much, she would have been at dinner this evening," Bridget retorted before she immediately apologized. "Sorry, Kathleen, you don't deserve me snapping at you. Thank you for trying to protect my feelings but I know what Maura is like. I will see you tomorrow morning. I missed you dreadfully, Kathleen. I can't wait to catch up properly."

Kathleen hugged her sister close.

"I missed you too and am so glad you are back."

CHAPTER 13

NEW YORK

*B*ella read the twins another story, they were rather unsettled this evening as she tucked them into bed. Or were they picking up on her mood? She loved the fact Bridget was back in New York. Kathleen was so excited and happy to see her sister. But what would the visit mean for Bella? Would Bridget agree with Kathleen's idea for Bella to travel with them to Riverside Springs?

She went downstairs to get a drink for Megan.

"What are you doing?" she asked as she

spotted Maura and Patricia in Lily's office, the door open.

"Mind your own business," Patricia snarled as she tried to push the door closed.

Over her shoulder, Bella saw the safe was open. Sarah was handing the contents to Maura who was putting the cash into a bag. She couldn't believe her eyes. Sarah, who was only thirteen, had been working at the sanctuary for over two years. She didn't live in, but Bella knew Lily had found her family a decent home and helped her to put her life back together. Sarah's mother had been working the streets. Sarah had been at risk of following her mam's footsteps until Lily gave them both a job at the sanctuary. Sarah's mam hadn't worked for a while due to illness, but Lily kept her on the payroll. She sent food parcels too. The girl and her mother owed Lily everything.

"Sarah, you can't do this to Lily. Not after everything she did for you."

Sarah gave her an ugly look. "She didn't do nothin' but take our money. She pays us a pittance while she lives in her brownstone. I've been a mug. Patricia showed me the truth. I should have been paid more and now I'm takin' what's mine. In my new life, I am going to earn more money than I know how to spend."

"Me too." Patricia glared at Bella.

"That's not yours. Some of that is the money Kathleen and I got from Mr. Hershel. Lily needs that to pay the bills." She turned to Maura. At least Kathleen's sister had the grace to look guilty, she didn't meet her eyes. "Maura, you know how much Lily does for us all. Not just us but the children on the streets. She helps people like Mrs. Fleming and others who can help more in the community. You can't steal from her."

"Don't listen to her, Maura. She took Kathleen away from you and left you with nothing." Patricia looked at her scornfully, "Just because no man would ever touch a cold-hearted witch like you, you can't bear for the rest of us to be happy. You stay here with your saintly Lily. Nobody else would want ya."

They pushed past her, Maura holding the bag.

"Come on, he won't wait forever," Patricia ordered as she shoved Bella to one side. Bella lost her footing and fell to her knees. It took a couple of seconds for her to untangle her skirts and get to her feet. She took off after them.

Spotting Maura in the gardens, Bella moved quicker than she thought possible. She grabbed the bag from Maura and threw it to the ground making the contents spill everywhere. Why had Lily not got someone to go to the bank? It was silly to keep so much money here. But she'd been distracted by Bridget's arrival. Everyone had. Sarah and Maura rushed to pick up the money, but the third woman turned her attention and hate on to Bella.

"Get her." Patricia lunged at her, she turned to run and came up against a hard chest. A man. Every inch of her body screamed as she realized a strange man was in front of her. She opened her mouth to scream but he had his hand there. He smelled disgusting, she didn't want to taste his vile skin. Her stomach roiled and she almost vomited.

"Get out of here now. Someone is bound to have heard and might have called the cops," he ordered.

"What about her?" Patricia asked.

"She won't tell anyone, will ya?" he leered at her, she tried to shake her head, but she couldn't move. Grinning, he released her so quickly she went falling back. She hit her head on something and the world turned black. Her last thought was she'd failed Kathleen. All their hard work had disappeared with that bag, and Kathleen had lost her sister too.

CHAPTER 14

NEW YORK

Kathleen returned to find the sanctuary in uproar. Mrs. Wilson was crying, something Kathleen had never seen the woman do. Stunned, she wished she hadn't told Mike to drop her at the gate. He was good to have around in times of trouble.

"What's going on? Why are you so upset, Mrs. Wilson?" she asked.

"Kathleen, I've failed Lily. I can't believe I didn't see what was going on right under my nose."

Kathleen drew the woman to a seat in the

hall and almost pushed her into the chair. Cook stood a little to one side, her hands flapping as much as her apron.

"Cook, perhaps you could get Mrs. Wilson a cup of tea with some sugar? Could you find Maura or Bella too and send them to us? Please."

Cook looked relieved to have someone take charge. "Can't find Maura, but I'll look for Bella, she was around here a few minutes ago." Cook's voice shook as much as Mrs. Wilson's.

Where was Maura? Her elder sister was never around when she was needed.

Kathleen rubbed Mrs. Wilson's shoulder until her sobs subsided. She couldn't make out what the woman was muttering about. Bella appeared, holding a stained cloth against the side of her head. Kathleen jumped to her feet.

"Let me look at your head," Kathleen said as she examined the other girl. She flinched at the size of the wound and the amount of blood. "You need the doctor. I'll send someone for Mike and Bridget. We have to leave Lily be."

Kathleen left Bella sitting with Mrs. Wilson as she ran to the door. She walked down to the gate and peered out onto the street looking up and down until she saw a couple of street urchins. She whistled to get their attention. Under any other circumstances she would have smiled at their surprise to see a woman dressed nicely whistling like a street rat.

"I need two runners. One to go for the doctor and the other to go to this address to get Mini Mike. You know him?"

The boys nodded.

"Here's a penny each and another one when you return. Please hurry."

The boys took off and she returned inside hoping her sister would come quickly.

Cook arrived back with tea. Running to the sewing room, she grabbed some white cloth and returned to Bella.

"Cook, I need some hot water," Kathleen ordered Cook who stared at the blood, looking whiter than her apron. "Cook, please hurry."

She hurried back to the hall, then checked

quickly on Mrs. Wilson before turning her attention to Bella, changing the stained cloth with a new one. She applied pressure to the wound, wishing she could remember what else she was supposed to do.

"Where were you? You know you're not supposed to go outside all alone." Kathleen took her anger out on the other girl.

"I tried to find a cop but there was no one around," Bella answered.

The police? What on earth had happened? Everything was fine when she'd left the sanctuary at noon.

"I was going to go to Miss Lily's house, but I couldn't remember where she lived," Bella explained. "I waited for you, but then I must have passed out as I woke up on the pavement."

Bella hiccupped which scared Kathleen almost as much as the wound. Bella never cried or showed much emotion over anything.

"Bella, what happened? Where's Maura?"

"I tried to warn her, but she wouldn't listen."

"Bella, calm down. You tried to warn who about what?" Kathleen wished Lily or Bridget were here.

"Your sister has gone. Patricia too. They took the money in the safe. Sarah went with them."

Kathleen sat back. "What?"

Bella held the cloth to her head, her eyes roving around the room, landing everywhere but on Kathleen's face. She wasn't lying, Kathleen could see. She was embarrassed.

"I don't blame you, Bella, I know my sister is extremely strong-willed. Now, what happened?"

Bella looked her in the eye. "They've gone. Patricia had a friend, a man. He told them they would make more money working for him than they would sewing, so they all left. They said the money was owed to them even though Patricia does less work than Maura. I tried to stop them, but they pushed me out of the way."

Bella took a deep breath. "I hit my head on something. Next thing I knew, I woke up on the pavement. I tried to stop them, I swear."

Kathleen drew the other girl close. "I know you did. I believe you."

The door opened as Bridget, Mike, Tommy, and the doctor all arrived at the same time. The doctor took over looking after Bella.

"Kathleen, what on earth is going on?" Bridget asked.

"Maura's gone with some of the other girls. Mrs. Wilson isn't making any sense. I think she must be in shock."

"But where have they gone?" Bridget asked as her husband followed her into the house.

"I don't know, Bridget. Bella said they went with some friend of Patricia's."

"Who is Patricia?" Carl asked.

"A horrible woman who came to the sanctuary a short time after Bridget left. She and Maura became very close. None of the rest of us liked her. She tells awful stories, and her and Maura used to sneak out at night. Maura always smelled funny the next day like she had been drinking."

The disgust on her sister's face made Kathleen take a step back.

"Kathleen Collins, you can't say things like that."

Annoyed, she retorted, "I can, if they're true. The money is missing too, Bridget. Bella says they took it and told her it was their wages."

"Maura wouldn't do something like that," Bridget said, her voice almost pleading. "Would she?"

Kathleen nodded grimly. "She's changed a lot. It began when David died and got worse when you left. I think Lily has been a saint, not throwing Maura out long ago. She has been so difficult to live with."

"Oh, this is bad. We'll have to involve the police," Bridget said, taking a seat.

"Doesn't Father Nelson have a friend who is a policeman? Maybe he can help us," Carl suggested. "I'll go and get him."

CHAPTER 15

NEW YORK

Carl left with Mini Mike. Bridget took charge of Mrs. Wilson, leading her into Lily's small sitting room and making sure she drank her tea. She seemed to be recovering from her shock. Bella's head wound wasn't dangerous, despite the amount of blood. The doctor said scalp wounds always bled a lot. He stitched the wound and showed them how to look after Bella.

"If you see any signs of infection, send for me at once," he said before Bridget paid him.

By the time the doctor left, Mrs. Wilson

had recovered enough to give a coherent account of what had happened. She had stayed later than usual as Lily had told her they were expecting a group of orphans who would stay at the sanctuary until the next train left. She was getting their rooms ready when she heard Patricia and Bella fighting. By the time she got downstairs, everyone had gone but she saw the safe was open and the money missing.

"I am so sorry, Bella," Mrs. Wilson said. "I thought you had left with them. I didn't think to go outside to check on you."

Bella didn't respond, but Kathleen ached for her friend.

"You were so brave, Bella. Who hit you?" Kathleen asked, hoping it wasn't Maura. It was bad enough stealing from Lily but to hit another woman, that was going too far.

"It was the man. He pushed me, and I fell and hit my head. They got away with everything. There was a lot more money in the safe due to our arrangement with the store owner. Mr. Hershel called today with payment and a bonus as well as an increased order. I was the one who told Maura. I was so excited. I guess pride does come before a fall."

Bridget looked totally confused. "Who is Mr. Hershel and why is he paying you money?"

"Bella and I found out that Mr. Hershel, a local store owner, was paying a middle man, Mr. Smithson, for the shirts the sanctuary produced. We asked him if we could supply him direct and he agreed. We split the money he was paying to Mr. Smithson between us and the store so both parties got a better deal."

Bridget's eyes filled with approval, making Kathleen feel better for a few minutes before she decided to come clean.

"Don't look at me, Bridget, it was Bella's idea. She has some brilliant plans to make money. None of which involve stealing," Kathleen hastily added as Bella looked crushed.

"Bella, none of this was your fault. You did your best to save the money and Sarah. What were Maura and Patricia thinking of? Sarah is barely thirteen years old." Kathleen saw the glance Bella and Bridget exchanged. She couldn't help feeling she was missing something. But Father Nelson's arrival with a policeman stopped all further conversation. Kathleen said she would go and settle the few children they had staying upstairs. Cook had taken them into the kitchen and was feeding them milk and cookies. Carl and Mini Mike had returned and joined Bridget and the others. Everyone had left Lily to sleep. It was bad enough she would hear the news the next day.

CHAPTER 16

NEW YORK

The next few days passed quickly. There was no sign of Maura or the other women. They had disappeared. Lily told Bella over and over it was not her fault. She reassured the younger girl that she had done her best, but Bella didn't believe her. Kathleen worried about her friend who was becoming increasingly down spirited.

She called to Lily's house to see Bridget. She and Carl were busy getting ready to take another group of orphans on the train. They planned on visiting Riverside Springs. Carl left to ask Cook for something so Kathleen seized her chance to speak to Bridget in private.

"Take Bella with you, please, Bridget. She needs to get away from New York."

"I was hoping you would come too, Kathleen."

"I have something else I need to do," Kathleen hedged, but she should have known Bridget wouldn't let the matter drop. Her sister stared at her and the silence lingered until it became uncomfortable.

"I want to find Shane and Michael. Before you say anything, I am old enough to travel alone. I'm nearly eighteen."

"You have just turned seventeen," Bridget corrected as Carl walked back into the room

"I am still old enough. In some places, women my age are married with children. Don't try to stop me, please, Bridget. I have to find the boys. With Maura gone, the feeling that I need to see them has only intensified."

Bridget exchanged a look with Carl before turning her attention back to Kathleen.

"Please, Bridget, I miss them so much. Especially Shane. We were always close, you know that."

"I know," Bridget answered. "But where will you look? If the boys wanted to stay in touch, they would have written."

Kathleen knew that was true but maybe they couldn't. She had to see for herself that Shane and Michael were doing well.

"I know they went to Iowa," she told Bridget.

"That's a large state. What if you wrote to various towns first? See if anyone knows of your brothers?" Carl asked her.

"No, that will take too long. I already spoke to Father Nelson. He is happy for me to accompany a Miss Gemma Screed, she is an experienced outplacement agent. I can help her with her charges while looking for the boys. Please don't stop me from going. I've saved enough for my ticket. I know you want to make sure they are happy too, Bridget."

Bridget sighed, telling Kathleen she was right.

"Please, Bridget, tell Father Nelson you don't object to my going. I will come to Riverside Springs once I have found Michael and Shane."

Kathleen saw Carl look at her, the understanding in his eyes making her feel like crying.

"And what if you don't find them?" he asked. "Have you thought about that?"

"Yes, but at least then I'll know I've tried," Kathleen said. "Mam wanted our family to stay together and look at us. Maura has run off, Annie and Liam are happy but are living with someone else, you're traveling all the time, Bridget. And the boys are off in Iowa."

"I won't stand in your way," Bridget conceded. "But promise me you will send for us or Charlie Doherty if you encounter any problems. I don't want any more heroics. Bella could have been seriously injured."

"Speaking of Bella, please look after her, Bridget. She has been a good friend to me since you left. That hard act you see is just that, an act. Underneath she has a loving heart."

Bridget didn't look convinced, but Kathleen knew her sister would do as she asked. She could trust her. "Bella is a wonderful seamstress, I thought she could take the position with Mrs. Grayson. Given what you said in your letters about the growing town and the lack of dressmaking skills, by the time I arrive in Riverside Springs there should be enough work for both of us. Assuming Mrs. Grayson agrees to our plan." Kathleen crossed her fingers, hoping her sister wouldn't question her assumptions. She had no idea whether there would be enough work for both her and Bella, but she knew she had to find her brothers. And Bella had to get out of New York. Her friend would thrive among people who treated her as she deserved to be treated, of that Kathleen was sure.

"Mrs. Grayson will be happy to help. She likes taking in those who are in need. She has a big heart and a mothering instinct. Doesn't she, Carl?"

Carl nodded.

"What will happen with Maura?" Kathleen asked quietly.

"Maura is a grown woman who made her own choices. It seems she has been keeping company with a man known to Mike and Tommy for a while now. They didn't know Maura was involved with him or they would have told Lily. They both feel bad about that."

Kathleen guessed Mike and Tommy didn't know the man because of his good deeds. Her heart was torn between anger at Maura and fear over what had happened to her and Sarah, the innocent in all of this.

"They shouldn't feel guilty," Kathleen said, her anger taking over. "I bet Maura doesn't. She didn't even try to help Bella."

"Mike and Tommy will work to find Sarah and get her back to Lily. Maybe we will be able to bring her to Riverside Springs at some point. But in the meantime, they may also find Maura. They can't force her to come back to the sanctuary as she is of age and thus..." Bridget shrugged her shoulders.

"They don't think Mr. Oaks is behind this, do they?" Kathleen voiced her fear aloud.

"No, Kathleen. That threat seems to have disappeared. He probably found something else to occupy him."

"How long do you think your trip will take?" Carl asked, perhaps purposely changing the subject. Kathleen smiled at him. Bridget had picked a good man.

"Father Nelson thinks it will be about three months in total. He's coming here later to collect me to go see a friend of his. You two should come as well. He is going to introduce me to Loring Brace, Charles Brace's son, who has taken over the Children's Aid Society. Father Nelson said Mr. Brace has some good ideas on how to make the orphan trains work better." She saw the glance the couple exchanged. "You two should come with me and meet Mr. Brace. You might find a willing ear for your ideas."

CHAPTER 17

NEW YORK

The meeting with Loring Brace went so well, Carl gave a delighted Kathleen tickets for Barnum's Circus. She decided to invite Bella. Her friend needed cheering up and anyway she wanted to talk to her about going to Riverside Springs. Lily insisted Mini Mike accompany the girls, she didn't want any more misadventures. Mike seemed to enjoy himself and took their good-natured teasing about how he could get a job in the circus, given his size, in his stride. They had a lovely day, and, on the way home, Kathleen decided it was a good time to ask Bella.

"You know I had an idea for us working together, Bella."

"Yes, you wanted us to go to Riversides Springs. Have you changed your mind?"

"Sort of."

At Bella's puzzled glance, Kathleen looked around to make sure nobody was listening to them.

"I want to find my brothers, Shane and Michael. I spoke to Loring Brace and he will help me get to Iowa. He is sending a group of orphans out there and said they need another helper."

"Oh, Kathleen, I am going to miss you so much. Are you sure you know what you are doing?"

Kathleen gave Bella a quick hug ignoring her friend's resistance. "I will miss you as well, but I have to do this. A voice inside my head is telling me to find them. Or at least try. But I need your help."

"I will do whatever I can," Bella said immediately.

"I still want us to set up our dressmaking shop like we discussed. I want you to go ahead of me and set everything up." She took a deep breath, "Bridget and Carl are heading back there next week, and they are happy for you to go with them. Mrs. Grayson—she owns the store—has offered to give me a discount on materials as she says I can only help increase store profits. People will come into the store looking for new dresses and buy ribbons and other items. What do you think?"

"Why are you so keen on getting me out of New York?" Bella asked.

"What do you mean, why? After what happened with Maura and before that. You deserve a better life. You and I are friends and I don't want to lose that. Also, you are a wonderful seamstress. We could have a nice business. We wouldn't be dependent on anyone, at least not after a while. Isn't it exciting?"

* * *

BELLA STARED AT KATHLEEN, not able to digest what she was saying. She couldn't believe anyone would want her to be their business partner. She was so overcome, she couldn't say a word.

"Bella, please say yes," Kathleen begged. "You know Lily won't throw you out on the street, but you might have to find a job. Especially with the baby on the way, Lily's husband might stop her from working at the sanctuary. Maura and her friends didn't help make it look like a safe place."

"Are you sure?" Bella asked. "I thought Bridget might have plans for you."

Kathleen turned bright red. "I have no idea what you mean."

"Yes, you do," Bella insisted. "You said she might want to marry you off."

"All the more reason you need to come. I'm not ready to marry anyone. I am far too young."

"Don't you want to have a family? I'd love to find someone special," Bella confided in a whisper, not wanting Mike to hear.

"Yes, someday, but not now. I want to find my brothers and work with you then... well, we'll see. I want to make sure you are taken care of. I don't want to leave you behind in New York."

Bella looked away.

"Bella?" Kathleen's tone faltered.

"I'm not sure I can, Kathleen. I went on the orphan train before. It was horrible."

"Yes, I know but that was a long time ago. This time it's different. You will have people you know, and you will have a job to go to. You don't have to live with anyone. Well, you will have to live in Mrs. Grayson's, but Bridget says she is an old dear."

Bella couldn't argue with Kathleen, but her friend didn't know her history. Nobody could want someone like her living with them. Lily was different. She understood, but most people wouldn't. Bella knew that from experience.

"Please say yes, Bella. I couldn't bear to leave you in New York."

Despite her misgivings, Bella nodded her head. She loved Kathleen like a sister. If she had been lucky enough to have a sibling, she would have wanted her to be like the girl beside her.

"If you won't do it for yourself or for me, do it for the children on the train. You know they are scared of leaving New York. You can relate to them as you traveled on an orphan train yourself" Kathleen urged.

"You are not playing fair, Kathleen Collins," she protested.

"So, will you go?" Kathleen asked her, not acknowledging what she had said. "Go on, what do you have to lose?"

Nothing. She had nothing to lose if she went and, maybe, she would find a happy ever after in a new town.

"Yes, I will go if Bridget and Carl are sure they don't mind me tagging along."

"They are sure." Kathleen squealed as she

hugged her close. This time, Bella hugged her friend back. She loved this girl like a sister.

"I hope you find your brothers, Kathleen. But…"

"But what?" Kathleen queried. "Go on, speak your mind."

"Just be prepared. There might be a good reason why they haven't made any effort to stay in touch." Bella hated the hurt in Kathleen's eyes, but she had to warn her. Not everyone's journey on the orphan train ended like a fairy tale.

CHAPTER 18

NEW YORK

When they arrived back from the circus, Kathleen saw Lily waiting for them. She looked distressed. There was no sign of Bridget and Carl.

"Sorry, Kathleen, Bella, I didn't mean to ruin your afternoon, but I had a visit this morning. Mr. Doyle came to see me."

"Who?" Bella asked.

"Megan and Eileen's father," Kathleen explained.

"The poor man returned to the Flemings to visit his children. He had been away trying to find work," Lily explained. "Seems he had heard of a lady called Helen Keller who herself is blind. She has set up The Industrial Home for the Blind in Brooklyn. It offers blind men shelter and work. He hoped to make enough money to give it to Mrs. Fleming to support his girls, but it didn't work out that way. At least not yet. The home will train him, but he can't see himself caring for the girls for a few years. Then he heard the news about Mrs. Fleming. He's asked us to put the twins on the orphan train. He wants them to find a good home, preferably together, although he knows that may not be possible."

"Oh no, poor Megan and Eileen," Kathleen said. "They desperately wanted him to come back. Have they seen him?"

"No, he thought it would be too upsetting and I guess I agree with him. They lost him then Mrs. Fleming, and now to see him again but not be able to live with him? It would be too hard," Lily explained.

"Oh, the poor family." Kathleen's heart

went out to both Mr. Doyle and his children. Life could be very unfair sometimes.

"He cried. I didn't know what to do. It's not like I could put my arms around him," Lily said, indicating her belly. "I asked Mini Mike to take him back to the home. At least he will be safe there."

"Who is Helen Keller?" Bella asked.

"A remarkable lady," Lily answered. "She is both blind and deaf, yet she learned how to talk and read. She is one determined lady. I think she will make a big difference to those men."

"But not in time for the girls," Bella added.

Kathleen waited for her friend to tell Lily their news. She hoped the fact the twins were going too would distract Bella from her own worries about the trip.

"It will be hard for the girls, but they are young and hopefully they will find a good home. I will ask Bridget to keep a close eye on them," Lily said.

"I am going to Riverside Springs. I will

look after them until they find new parents," Bella said, causing Lily to look at her. Her shocked expression gave way to a large smile.

"You are? Oh, I am so happy for you, Bella. I think leaving New York will do you the world of good. Plenty of fresh air and nice people in Riverside Springs from what Bridget says," Lily said excitedly as she patted the chair beside her.

Kathleen hung back and let Bella tell Lily about their plans. She noted the excitement creeping into Bella's face. Maybe her friend would be able to face her fears after all.

CHAPTER 19

KATHLEEN

athleen walked into the sanctuary kitchen where Bridget and Carl were helping pack some food baskets for the train.

"Bridget, Carl, I have something to tell you," she said, waiting for them to look at her. "Bridget, I am going to find Shane and Michael."

"Yes, I know, you told us your plans already," Bridget said, looking confused.

"No, I mean, I am going tomorrow. Before you argue with me, I have secured a position with the Children's Aid Society. I am to accompany a Miss Screed and a group of orphans looking for new homes. Loring Brace was kind enough to listen to my quest and is fairly confident I will be able to find the boys."

"Oh, Kathleen, tomorrow? Are you sure you know what you are doing? Carl and I discussed going looking for them, but we have so many orphans who need our help..." Bridget looked so distressed, Kathleen was almost sorry she had decided on this course of action. She hugged her close.

"I have to go, Bridget. Maura leaving and Mrs. Fleming dying showed me just how short life is. Before I can settle down and make a life of my own, I want to be sure the boys are happy. I think Mam would have wanted me to do this."

"I am sure she would. You are a wonderful young lady. She would be very proud of you," Carl commented as Bridget seemed to have lost the ability to speak.

"Thank you, Carl. Please look after both

Bridget and Bella for me. I will write to you care of Mrs. Grayson's mercantile."

"Make sure you do, or I just might follow you to Iowa." Bridget threatened before adding, "Don't do anything reckless, Kathleen."

"I won't. I promise."

KATHLEEN WAS ALMOST REGRETTING her decision to try to find her brothers. Miss Screed was fifty if she was a day, had never married and, what was worse, she seemed to hate children. All of them, not just those in her care. Her hard-pinched face never showed any emotion other than disapproval. She looked older than her years with her greying hair screwed up in a tight bun, possibly fashionable sometime before the Civil War era, Kathleen thought uncharitably. She seemed to consider the orphans in her care a burden. When the passengers on the train complained about the noise some of the younger children were making, she took the side of the passengers. She threatened the children with severe punishment if they didn't stop crying and carrying on as she called it.

"I don't know why you entertain their tears," Miss Screed said to Kathleen. "They're little brats, each and every one of them. They should be thankful we are taking them to live elsewhere."

Kathleen counted to ten in her head before she answered. It wouldn't help anyone if she were to fall out with this woman.

"They're children. It's only normal they would miss their families."

Miss Screed adjusted her black traveling dress, the voluminous material covering most of the seat. "Miss the people who beat them or sold them on the streets? Miss Collins, your youth may account for your innocence but don't let these children fool you. They would murder you in your bed if you gave them half a chance. That group over there came direct from New York prison."

Kathleen wanted to scream at her that the children weren't deaf, they heard every comment the woman said.

"Yes, but only because that was the only home available for them," Kathleen said. "These children haven't committed any crime other than that of being poor. What possessed you to want to work with orphans with your views?"

"You are impertinent and rude," Miss Screed shot back. "It is a good thing your parents are dead. They would be ashamed to call you their daughter."

Kathleen refused to let the horrid woman see how much her words hurt. Instead, she vowed to ignore her. She wouldn't change the woman's opinion, so it was pointless trying.

"Right old battleaxe, ain't she?" A boy of about twelve said to her as she soothed a young child to sleep.

"Show some respect, Patrick Hayes" Kathleen whispered, glancing at the older woman to see if she had heard.

"Why? Just because she's older and has more money than me? Someday, just you wait and see, I'll make my fortune and have people like her bow down to me."

Kathleen had to fight back a smile. He was a right cheeky young man but, having worked on the streets of New York, one had to be quick-witted to survive.

"I hope things work out very well for you, Patrick, but your dream shouldn't be to make other people subservient. What do you hope to do when you are older?" she asked him.

"I want to be a reporter. To tell the world the truth about what happens in our country. I had a good job in New York, but they rounded me up and threw me in jail. Judge gave me the choice of going to the Tombs or going out West."

"What job did you have?" Kathleen asked. It wasn't unusual for innocent children to get caught up in a mass arrest, but it wasn't that common either. Miss Screed had told her

Patrick had been arrested several times for pickpocketing and other illegal activities.

"I was a newspaper boy. I was good at it too as I can read. My ma taught me before she ran off with me baby brother." He looked at her as if daring her not to believe him.

Kathleen wondered why the mother had taken one child and not the other, but she didn't want to hurt him by asking.

"Maybe you'll get a job at a newspaper office," she suggested. "I'll see if I can do anything."

"Nobody will want me, not when Lady Muck over there tells them her version of what I did. I swear to you, miss, I never took nothing from no one."

"I will do my best, Patrick, I promise. But for now, try to get along with Miss Screed. She is in charge after all."

She had to suppress a giggle as he stuck his tongue out at the older woman.

CHAPTER 20

KATHLEEN

athleen did her best to make the journey pleasant for the children. When the train stopped to take on fuel and water, she took them outside to run around and burn up some of their energy. On the train, she taught them different games to try to pass the time. Nothing she did earned her any praise from Miss Screed, but at least the older woman left her and the children alone.

The first town they came to, Miss Screed led the children out of the train, telling them to smile and be quiet. "There are some people here who might want to adopt you."

Kathleen smiled at the children, hoping to instill some confidence in them. They walked a little way into town to find someone had set up a picnic on the green. There was a band to play music and banners flying overhead.

"What do they say?"

"They say 'Orphans welcome here,' Susie. These people want to welcome us to their town."

Susie smiled, as did many of the children. The townsfolk were friendly and handed out plates of food and glasses of water and lemonade. Kathleen watched as the children gravitated toward different couples. She burst out laughing as one of the men grabbed one of the younger boys and twirled him up in the air. The child squealed with laughter. Miss Screed looked on in disapproval, but thankfully nobody paid her any notice. The afternoon passed quickly and by the time they returned to the train, they had found homes for over ten orphans.

"That was a nice place, wasn't it?" Patrick asked Kathleen as he helped her climb back onto the train.

"Yes, it was. I'm sorry you didn't meet a family," she replied, giving his hair a quick rub.

"Who would take that ragamuffin?" Miss Screed said as she brushed past.

Patrick stuck his tongue out at her retreating back. Kathleen couldn't blame him, she was tempted to do the same.

The next couple of towns, whilst not as welcoming as the first one, also accepted orphans so the numbers in their care dwindled as they traveled farther. At every town, Kathleen made enquiries, but nobody seemed to have met her brothers. She was beginning to believe she had gone on a wild goose chase. That night she couldn't sleep properly, an ominous feeling keeping her awake.

CHAPTER 21

BELLA

*B*ella couldn't believe she was leaving New York on another orphan train. She tried to hide her nervousness so as to not scare the younger children.

"This time it will be different, Bella, I promise," Bridget reassured her. "Mrs. Grayson is a wonderful woman. She will help you find plenty of customers as a seamstress, as it will benefit her store if you are able to sell dresses. Grayson's is the only store in the area to carry material."

Bella didn't respond. Bridget looked at her

closely, "You have a real gift with design. Those dresses you made for the twins are wonderful. The grey-blue material is practical, and those hats are just to die for."

Bella smiled as she looked over at the twins. Megan and Eileen had been thrilled with their new clothes. They had told her it was the first time they ever had a new dress. She'd bought the material on impulse and when she saw the hats on a secondhand good's stall, she had to have them. By adding a piece of the dress material, they looked like new.

"I thought it might help them find a family together," Bella confided in a whisper to Bridget.

"You are so thoughtful, Bella, but you hide those feelings by pretending to be cold and indifferent. Let people in Riverside Springs see the real you. Especially Mrs. Grayson."

Bella bit her lip, wondering how much Bridget remembered about their conversation when she'd tried to persuade Bridget not to let Annie go on the orphan train.

"But what if she doesn't approve of me?" Bella asked. "You know, with my history?"

"Bella, your story is yours to tell. Nobody else knows any details. I haven't shared anything with anyone, except Carl. I don't keep secrets from my husband but, trust me, he will not tell a soul."

Bella saw Bridget was sincere, but she found it hard to believe people didn't know what she was just by looking at her.

"Bella, you need to put the past behind you if you can. Try to think of everyone in Riverside Springs as being like Kathleen. You showed my sister a different, nicer side. Put that on display and you will have no problems at all."

It was easy for Bridget to say that, but she had no idea how hard it was to pretend to be something she wasn't. Like an innocent young woman who had something decent to bring to a community. Bella took out her sewing. Working with her hands relaxed her and gave her time to think. She wondered how Kathleen was getting on with her quest.

Bella tried to keep her fears under control. She was seventeen years old, not a vulnerable child. Nobody was going to adopt her or force her to live with them. She didn't have to worry about being beaten, yet her nightmares of her early years had come back with a vengeance. It was difficult to sleep on the hard seats on the train but, even when she did close her eyes, she could only see the whip. She must have nodded off as she woke with a start. Someone was standing over her. She shrunk back.

"Bella, it's Bridget. You were crying out in your sleep. Are you okay?" Kathleen's sister said, leaning in from the aisle.

Mortified she had been caught crying, Bella wiped at her cheeks and nodded. "It was just a bad dream."

Instead of walking away, Bridget took a seat beside her forcing Bella to move over.

"I know you had a horrible time when you were little, but this will be different. If you don't like Riverside Springs, you can save up your wages and go somewhere else. Back to New York if you want. Lily would never see you homeless."

Bella knew Bridget was trying to be kind, but it wasn't that simple.

"I seem to bring trouble to Lily." She seemed to bring trouble to everyone, but Bella left those words unspoken.

"Bella, you are not to blame for the money being stolen. You tried to stop Maura and Patricia and look what happened," Bridget said. "You're too hard on yourself."

A child crying caught Bridget's attention. She glanced up the car before looking back into Bella's eyes. She patted Bella's hand. "I have to go, but please remember we are here for you. Kathleen made me promise to look after you."

Bella smiled at the reference to Kathleen. She wondered how her friend was faring. She closed her eyes to try to sleep but it was no use. She opened them to find the Doyle twins,

Megan and Eileen, staring at her. Both were sucking their thumbs.

"Sorry, girls, did I wake you as well? I had a bad dream," she explained quickly, not wanting to upset the girls. If they started crying, the whole car could start.

"Did your mama leave you, too?" Megan asked her.

"Not recently. Are you having trouble sleeping?" she asked, trying to change the subject.

The six-year-olds nodded their heads although Eileen yawned.

"Would you like me to tell you a story?" she offered.

"Yes, please, Pa used to do that. He couldn't read as his eyes didn't work, but he knew lots of stories," Megan told her.

Bella knew a little of the girls' stories. Their mother and youngest brother had disappeared. She told the girls stories about princes and princesses. She made up the details, but they didn't seem to care. Soon they were fast asleep. She hadn't noticed Bridget was listening in too.

"You're a natural mother, Bella. Someday, when you find someone special, you will have a lovely family."

Bella didn't know how to react. It was a nice thing for Bridget to say if she meant it, but was she teasing her? Bridget had to know the chances of anyone decent wanting to marry a girl like her were low. She closed her eyes and pretended to be asleep.

CHAPTER 22

BELLA

*B*ella knew the last train stop would be Green River, after which they would take the stagecoach to Riverside Springs. But first, they had to stop at a town called Mud Butte. Bella hoped the town would be prettier than its name. She held Megan and Eileen's hands tightly as the little group walked to the town hall. Bridget was still hopeful the twins would find a home together, but it wasn't looking good. Nobody at any of the previous stops had offered both girls a home.

Bella had overheard Bridget and Carl

talking about the financial depression, and while she didn't understand all of what they said, she knew unemployment rates were increasing around America.

"Do you think we will find a nice place to live, Bella?" Megan asked, looking up at her.

"Yes, of course you will," Bella lied through her teeth. She could only hope these young girls didn't endure the terrors she had. She glanced around the room at the small group of people waiting to meet the orphans. Even now, her skin was crawling as the sweat fell from her shoulder blades. Her breathing was too rapid, and she felt she would faint. But she had to push her own feelings aside for the sake of these girls.

"Good morning, everyone. Thank you for coming today and for your interest in our children," Carl said as he took center stage, Bridget standing to his right.

"Any of them got experience in farm work? I need some good workers," a man wearing dirty overalls said, stepping closer to the stage.

"The children have all had a little training at the industrial school before joining the train. But coming from the city areas of New York, none have any actual farming experience," Bridget answered, her tone calm but her expression showing irritation at the man's attitude. Bella admired the other woman. She wanted to scream at the man to open his eyes and see the group as individual children not a workforce to be exploited.

"I'd like a young girl, please. We don't have much, and she would have to help around the house, but we will send her to school and give her a good home," a rather worn-out-looking woman said as she came forward. Bella watched Bridget's reaction as the woman reached out to Megan who took a step back, her hand tightly holding that of her sister.

"We don't have any other girls. Only the twins. Megan is a lovely girl and a hard worker. She is bright and intelligent too but has fallen behind at school due to her family circumstances. We would prefer one family took both girls. Being twins they do not want to be separated," Bridget said to the woman, her tone soft and gentle.

Bella looked at the woman closely. She seemed torn between her desire for Megan and the reality of taking both children.

"Gracie, you know we can't take both. We haven't got the money," a man, she guessed the woman's husband, stepped forward. He swiped the hat from his head as he addressed himself to Bridget.

"Giles MacDonagh is the name, and this here is my wife Gracie. We lost our own little girl to the fever last year. I got a smallholding outside town. We get by, but we just can't afford two extra mouths. I'm sorry."

"We won't eat a lot, will we, Eileen? Please, mister, we will be good and work hard for you. We have to stay together. We just have to," Megan begged the man.

Bella looked away, not because of Megan's begging but the look on the couple's face. They were almost as heartbroken as the girls.

"I am sorry, but we can't. Come on, Gracie, let's be going home."

The woman tore her gaze from Megan and walked out of the room with slumped shoulders, her husband wrapping his arm around her waist in support. Megan stared after them, her expression telling Bella the girl now knew the chances of her and Eileen going to the same home were next to zero.

CHAPTER 23

KATHLEEN

Kathleen's nose itched as the smell of burning wood woke her. She opened her eyes to find black smoke pouring into the car.

"Fire, fire." The conductor's voice echoed through the terror of children screaming.

Leaping to her feet, she thanked God the train had stopped. Opening the door carefully, she lowered each child out onto the ground, directing the older children to take the younger ones to a point of safety where other passengers had gathered.

"Careful now, take the little ones by the hand. Make sure you stay together. Leave your bags behind. Don't let anyone wander off," she repeated over and over. She kept going through the car until she was sure the fifteen remaining orphans were safely off.

Many of the men from the car had run to help put out the fire, while some had stayed to help the rest of the passengers disembark. Miss Screed was one of the last to leave the car, having insisted on gathering up her belongings. She was just stepping down from the open door when a gust of wind sent a flash of orange toward her. Her costume went up in flames faster than a candle wick. Kathleen stood rooted to the spot as the fire threatened to engulf the older woman. From the corner of her eye, she saw someone come running. He tackled Miss Screed, sending her tumbling to the ground, and rolled her over and over. The flames were extinguished by the time another man came running with some water.

"Miss Screed, are you all right?" the conductor asked the older woman. She appeared to be fine, if a little shaken after her ordeal. Kathleen was more interested in Patrick, the boy who had saved her. She caught him staring at his blackened hands. Pushing the passengers out of the way, she grabbed him and thrust his hands in the bucket of cold water. "Keep them in there, it will help dull the pain. You were so brave. I'm very proud of you," Kathleen told him. The crowd gathered around them with people pushing to see what had happened. She spotted Miss Screed coming forward, fully expecting her to thank Patrick for saving her life.

"I want this boy arrested. He tried to kill me," the old lady demanded.

"Miss Screed, he saved your life," Kathleen protested just as loudly. "You could have burnt to death if he hadn't acted so quickly."

"Nonsense, it was only a tiny flame which I was about to put out myself. Until I was thrown to the ground and manhandled in such an undignified manner. I want him arrested. Goodness knows why the New York prison authorities released him in the first place." Miss Screed sounded hysterical. "I want him put in irons until we reach the next town where he is to be handed over to the sheriff."

The crowd's mutterings grew louder. Kathleen looked from the group of orphans standing at the sidelines, their eyes wide open, taking everything in, to Patrick, his red-raw hands suspended in cold water. The poor boy was shivering, possibly from shock.

"The boy needs a doctor. He's a hero. Please, is anyone a doctor?" Kathleen addressed the crowd.

"You called for a doctor?" a well-dressed gentleman said. He didn't seem aware of what had happened.

Kathleen nodded. She put her arm around Patrick's shoulders, fearing he would fall over. He was shaking violently at this point.

"My friend, Patrick, just saved this woman's life but at great cost to himself. He used his bare hands to put out the flames. They seem badly burned."

The doctor took charge, telling the conductor he needed some space on the train to examine the boy. His cultured accent and fine clothes made the conductor respond quickly, Kathleen noticed.

Josie Smith, a fourteen-year-old orphan, took charge of the rest of the orphans. The fire had been put out and the conductor deemed it safe to return to the cars. Kathleen went with Patrick. She didn't care where Miss Screed went so long as it was far away from her. She didn't trust herself to deal with the woman just now.

THE DOCTOR first washed his own hands before gently examining Patrick's.

"Can you pass me my bag please, miss?" the doctor asked her, raising his eyebrows.

"Collins, Kathleen Collins," she replied,

handing him his bag which the conductor had left on the chair beside her. The car was obviously first class, the seats luxurious compared to the plain wooden ones she and Patrick were used to.

"Richard Green is my name. I will give you something to help with the pain, young man. Then I will apply this salve to the skin. You will need to keep your hands covered with clean bandages. Infection is our enemy. We must do everything we can to avoid it."

"Yes, doctor," Kathleen answered as Patrick seemed to have lost his voice.

"You are an extremely brave young man. Your mother must be very proud of you both."

Kathleen blushed at the misunderstanding, but Patrick quickly jumped in to explain.

"I ain't got a ma or a pa. I'm an orphan and Miss Collins works for the group that is taking us out west to find families."

"Ah, I see," the doctor replied, giving Kathleen an appraising look.

"Who was the lady you saved?" the doctor asked. "She should be very grateful."

Kathleen couldn't control her reaction.

"She wants him arrested," she said crossly. "She insists he tried to kill her. Patrick and Miss Screed haven't seen eye to eye this whole journey, but he meant no harm. He was genuinely trying to help her."

"Of course, he was. Only a fool would think different. Perhaps I should speak to this Miss Screed." For all his nice clothes and accent, he didn't seem to judge them and find them wanting.

"Would you?" Kathleen asked, feeling hopeful. "That would be kind of you as she pays no attention to me."

"I shall speak to the lady. Perhaps you could accompany me?" He directed the question to Kathleen before turning his attention to Patrick. "This is my car, so make yourself comfortable. You may feel a little sleepy after the laudanum I gave you. I will be back soon, but you are safe here, young man. I won't let anyone hurt you, let alone arrest you. You have my word for it."

"Thank you, sir," Patrick mumbled, his voice already sounding groggy. Kathleen helped the boy lie across the seat, removing his shoes so they wouldn't mark the fine fabric.

The doctor draped a blanket over him. "His body needs to adjust to the shock."

Kathleen led the way down through the cars to where Miss Screed should be sitting. Before they reached her, she stopped.

"Doctor Green, there is something you should know. It would appear Patrick had a run-in with the police before he joined this train. Miss Screed seems to believe him capable of murder. I do not share those beliefs." Kathleen took a deep breath. She wasn't sure if what she was about to say was the truth as she had no proof but her own instinct. "I think Patrick stole some food because he was starving. I know stealing is a crime, but I do not believe he is capable of any serious wrongdoing."

"I am sure you are right, Miss Collins. A

boy who shows bravery like he did is hardly the type to commit murder." The doctor looked pensive. "It's amazing how uncharitable some people are when it comes to dealing with the poor. Thank you for warning me."

CHAPTER 24

BELLA

*B*ella wondered how Kathleen was faring. She wasn't sure how much more of these interviews with prospective parents she could take. She wanted to keep the twins with her, not give them to a stranger.

"Bridget, couldn't we take the girls to Riverside Springs with us? I'm a hard worker, I can take in enough sewing to provide for us all," Bella whispered to Bridget, not wanting the girls to hear her.

"No, you can't, Bella. I appreciate your offer and the thinking behind it, but the girls need a stable home. They need parents, a roof over their heads, and the chance to go to school."

Bella was about to protest but Bridget hadn't finished. "Bella, you need to be free to pursue your own dreams. Believe me, I understand. I couldn't bear to give up Annie and Liam either. But we have to do what is best for the children."

Bella nodded. It had been a silly idea anyway. She didn't know if she would earn enough to support herself, let alone two children. She moved back to where the remaining orphans stood waiting.

Two men came forward. Bella looked at them suspiciously as they addressed Bridget.

"Morning, ma'am. My name is Joe Maitland, and this here is my brother Jack. We own adjoining places just outside of town and are looking to take in some orphans."

They smiled and acted all mannerly, but there was something about them that made

Bella feel uneasy. But she couldn't put her finger on exactly why that was.

"Thank you for your interest, Mr. Maitland, but we don't allow single men to adopt children. We are looking for families," Bridget said politely but firmly.

"Sorry, ma'am. I understand that. We are both married. Rebecca and Alice couldn't bear to come here in case we didn't find anyone. My missus, she has a big heart and would want to take them all in. But we can only afford one each. I know the girls are twins, but I was wondering if you, or they, would consider coming to us. They would live near to one another and could see each other every week."

"Every week?" Bridget echoed, which told Bella she was considering it.

"We know it's not ideal, ma'am, but it's the best we can do. We came on the orphan trains too about ten years after the war ended. There were eight of us. We all got separated but me and Jack, well we got to stay in the same town.

We kept close. We never got to meet any of the rest of our family again."

Judging by the expression on his face, Carl was considering their offer. Bridget looked less convinced. Bella held her breath.

"That's the truth, ma'am," Jack chimed in. "We both have young'uns at home. Joe, he got a boy and a girl. I got two boys and I had a girl, but she died in the influenza epidemic. Alice, my missus, got real sick. She's better now but we won't have any more children." Jack's fingers tugged at his collar as his cheeks flushed. "We will make sure the girls go to school and church. They will have chores to do, but nothing more than our own children. What do you think?"

Bella heard the intake of breath and her attention shifted to Megan and Eileen who had been listening closely to the men. She saw the girls huddle together, Megan talking rapidly, Eileen just shaking her head. Perhaps if the girls were separated, Eileen might talk for herself. The random thought surprised Bella.

"Thank you for your offer, gentlemen. I must admit it seems like a good solution given the lack of alternatives. Perhaps we could bring the girls out to meet your families. Then we could make a final decision?" Carl asked, but his tone suggested they had to agree if they wanted to take the children.

The men exchanged glances, but Carl was in her line of vision, so she couldn't read their expressions. Bridget had moved to the other side of the hall.

"That would be right fine with us. We could give you a ride out today if you had the time."

"Let me go check with my wife. I will be right back. Bella, please stay with the girls."

Bella nodded. She saw the men glance at her, but she didn't make eye contact. She moved closer to the young girls.

"Bella, can't you tell them we want to stay together?" Megan asked, her wide eyes making Bella feel even worse.

"I can't do that, Megan sweetheart. I think they would if they could but…"

"I know, they don't have enough money for two of us. Nobody does."

Bella hated the words, but they were the truth. She looked up just in time to catch Jack Maitland's gaze roving over her. She shuddered at the expression in his eyes, but it was gone so quickly she wondered if she had imagined it. She wanted to run back to the train and get out of Mud Butte.

But Megan was holding her hand.

"Will you come with us, Bella? To see where they live?" Megan asked her, lisping slightly. Eileen stared at her, a begging expression in her eyes, but she stayed silent as usual.

"I don't think I would be allowed," Bella started to say, but as Megan's gaze dropped she changed her mind. These girls needed her. "I will ask Bridget. Stay here, I will be right back."

CHAPTER 25

BELLA

*B*ella walked slowly over to where Bridget and Carl were talking to a man. As she got closer, she saw his sheriff's badge. Her stomach churned. Was there trouble?

"Bella, this is Sheriff Bell," Carl introduced her to the man. "He was just telling us the Maitlands are wonderful people. They have given homes to orphans in the past."

Funny how they didn't mention that earlier, Bella thought, but she didn't say anything. The Sheriff was looking at her closely. She forced a smile in greeting before asking Bridget if she could come to the farms with her.

"I don't think there is any need for that is there? I have vouched for the families," the sheriff replied before Bridget could answer.

"The girls would like me to come. Seems easy to grant them a simple request, especially if you are going to split them up," Bella surprised herself by saying. In the past she would have been quaking in her boots.

"Of course, you can come, Bella. Please excuse us, Sheriff," Bridget said, taking Bella's elbow and leading her back to the girls. They left Carl speaking to the lawman.

"Something doesn't feel right," Bella whispered as they walked across the hall. Bridget rubbed her hand across her forehead. "Bridget, what's wrong?"

"Sorry, Bella, I feel a little unwell."

"Can I get you some water?"

"Yes, please. I think I will sit down for a few minutes too as the room is spinning." Bridget sat as Bella went to find water. She came back, relieved to see Bridget didn't look as pale as before. Her friend sipped the water before saying, "Bella, we discussed this. The girls have to find homes. It's not ideal, but at least they would be close to each other."

"It's not that. I don't trust those men," Bella insisted, after glancing around to make sure nobody was listening to her.

Bridget stopped drinking to stare at her. "I know you had a horrible time, but you can't let your bad experience color your judgement. Let's go and see the Maitland families before making a final decision."

Bella nodded, wondering if she was letting her past take over. She waited for Bridget to finish but when she stood, she had to sit down again quickly.

"Sorry, Bella, but could you get Carl for me, please?"

Bella hurried away and found Bridget's husband. He took one look at Bridget and insisted on taking her to see a doctor. Bridget refused but did agree to Carl securing a hotel room, saying a rest in a real bed would do her good.

Bella went to check on the girls who were sucking some candy.

"I hope you don't mind, but we gave the girls a little treat," Joe said with a smile on his face.

"I hope you said thank you, girls," Bella said quickly.

"They did, ma'am. Lovely manners they have. My missus is going to just love them." Joe grinned at her, showing his lack of teeth. She suppressed the shudder running down her spine.

Yet he sounded so sincere, Bella thought Bridget must be right even if the hair on the back of her neck wouldn't sit down.

"Mrs. Watson is feeling unwell, so her husband will come to the farm with us," she told them.

"I hope she will recover soon. I have some goods to buy at the store so will come back to collect you in two hours' time. Will that suit?"

Bella nodded. She wanted him to leave and take her feelings of discomfort with her.

"I am glad you are coming, Bella, but I hope Bridget will be okay," Megan said, once she was alone with the girls again.

"I'm sure she'll be just fine," Bella reassured the little girl.

The hours passed quickly as the orphaned boys found homes with different people. Bella knew some were looking for farm workers, but they seemed like decent people. She had no way of knowing whether they would treat the boys right. She had to trust her gut instinct as she was the only one left to make a decision. Carl had yet to return. By the time he did, there was only the twins and a couple of boys aged ten and twelve left.

"Carl, may I speak with you please?"

"Certainly, Bella, what's on your mind? You did a wonderful job while I was with Bridget?" he said, looking down at the list she had given him of who had adopted the boys.

"It's about the twins, Megan and Eileen. I…"

"Yes?" he queried, his expression distracted.

She didn't want to annoy him. "I hope you don't mind me saying this, but I don't like the Maitlands."

"Why? Have they done something?"

"No, not exactly. I can't really explain it, but I think it would be best if you didn't let them take the twins."

A look of understanding came over his face and she sighed with relief.

"I know you find this difficult, Bella, but the fact is, the twins need a new home. Megan and Eileen have grown attached to you, but they are young, and they will adapt. I am sure everything will work out just fine."

"No, I mean, yes, they need homes but not with these people. Can't we try at the next station?"

"We can if their property is not suitable or we have a real reason to doubt the merits of the placement. I am sorry, Bella, but I have to think of everyone. What is best for the twins and for Bridget. The strain of this journey is taking its toll. I'm sure you understand."

Whether she did or didn't wasn't relevant. It was obvious the topic was closed for discussion. She could only hope something about the Maitlands property made them unsuitable parents. Carl was doing his best for those he loved, and she knew he wouldn't place the girls in danger. He was right, they didn't have any proof against the Maitlands apart from her gut instinct. Who was she to decide whether a home was good enough or not?

CHAPTER 26

KATHLEEN

athleen and Dr Green found Miss Screed telling a group of people about her ordeal. She had changed into a new traveling costume, it seemed to be the match of the first one she had worn. The black made her look more severe and older than her years. Kathleen realized she hated the woman and was amazed at the depth of her feelings.

"Miss Screed, would you like me to examine you, although you seem to have escaped serious injury?" The doctor smiled at the outplacement agent, but Kathleen saw his eyes remained cold.

Miss Screed looked up with a smile at the cultured accent. Kathleen wanted to scream at the woman. Just because someone spoke well and was dressed nicely didn't make them a better person. Although the doctor seemed kind and very caring.

"I am quite well aside from some bruising. Thank you, Doctor, for asking. My injuries don't need attending, no thanks to that ruffian. I assume he is now under lock and key."

"On the contrary, he is asleep in my car. The poor boy may lose the use of his hands. I believe him to be a hero. He saved you from serious injury, perhaps even from death. You should be grateful, Miss Screed. Someone else in his position may not have bothered."

The crowd gasped. Miss Screed opened and closed her mouth numerous times, but she didn't get a word out.

"I don't know who you think you are, Doctor, but you are operating outside of your authority. These children are in my care and I shall escort them to their destination." Miss Screed stood her ground and, for once, Kathleen had a little admiration for the woman. She didn't scare easily but it was a pity she didn't use that bravery for the children in her care.

"I am Richard Green, my grandfather being Charles Green."

Kathleen had no idea who that was but, judging by the look on the older woman's face, she recognized the name.

"My grandfather brought me up to believe all men are created equal. That applies to children too, no matter their background. My grandfather contributed a significant amount of money to various charities, including, I am sure, the one you are employed by. Believe me, they will be hearing my version of what took place here, and it will not show you in a good light."

He turned to look at Kathleen, "I must return to my patient. Miss Collins, if you would accompany me please. You can tell me about the plans for this group of children." The doctor moved away before stopping and turning back to the conductor. "Before I forget, can you please see that every child in the group gets a decent meal? You can bill me for it. They have witnessed a terrible thing and are bound to be suffering the effects. Thank you."

He moved away before the conductor reacted. Kathleen followed in his wake, bemused as people moved out of his way as he made his way through the car. It was true what they said about money talking.

As they neared his car, he stopped once more.

"Miss Collins, please forgive my bragging back there. I never tell people who I am. I believe people who have to point out their wealth are quite vulgar. But given the circumstances, I think it was appropriate. I just hope you don't think less of me."

She opened her mouth and closed it again a couple of times. Standing this close, she saw he was older than she had first thought. Probably late twenties if she was to hazard a guess.

"Not at all, sir. I mean, Doctor," she stuttered.

"My name is Richard, but if you don't believe it is appropriate for you to call me by my given name, 'doctor' will do fine. Now, let's see if our young patient is awake, shall we?"

"Doctor, did you mean it when you said he might lose the use of his hands?" she asked tentatively, not wanting to suggest he'd been lying, but hoping he had exaggerated.

"That all depends on the next forty-eight hours. If infection doesn't set in, then he should heal very well. Though he will likely be left with some scars."

CHAPTER 27

KATHLEEN

Kathleen took a deep breath when she saw Patrick. Judging by his pallor and expression, Patrick was in severe pain, but he never complained. Not once. Richard applied the salve again and again. He changed the bandages every four hours, explaining he did so to avoid infection. Then he showed Patrick how to exercise his hands so that he would retain maximum use of his fingers. The passengers got off at the next stop which was another small town. Josie told Kathleen, Doctor Green had insisted on buying all the children some candy as well as fruit from the store.

"He is ever so nice, Miss Collins, ain't he? Wonder what it is like to be so rich?" Josie said, sighing as she gazed at the doctor.

Kathleen hurried the young girl back onto the car. Then she heard the doctor calling for her. She adjusted her shawl before she walked back toward him.

"I have wired ahead for more supplies. They should be waiting for us at the next stop I hope. I need some more ointment for his hands, but I am hopeful we are past the critical stage."

"Thank you, Doctor, for looking after him so well."

"It is my pleasure, Miss Collins. I find him very amusing. He is quick-witted, intelligent and, if circumstances were different, I am sure he would have a wonderful range of careers open to him. I think he would make a wonderful lawyer given his ability to argue on every topic."

Kathleen laughed. Patrick certainly didn't keep his opinions to himself.

He seemed to have blossomed since the doctor insisted he travel with him. Miss Screed had recovered from her "ordeal" as she called it. Kathleen was relieved she wouldn't be called upon to make decisions regarding the placement of the children. She didn't relish having to organize the meetings with prospective parents. She wasn't sure she would be able to hand over any of the children, they had all become like a family.

Miss Screed had adjusted her attitude, at least slightly. She wasn't as hurtful or mean to the children, although she continued to ignore them. Doctor Richard made up for it. He visited the group regularly and, because of his visits, the other passengers, not to mention the conductor, seemed to see the children in a better light too. Kathleen couldn't help being upset the children were not being treated better because of their own worth but because a "gentleman" had taken an interest in them. It was simply amazing what money and position could achieve. She wondered how Bella was faring on her train journey? Was she learning more about human nature too?

188

CHAPTER 28

BELLA

*A*ll too soon for Bella's liking, Joe Maitland returned to say the wagons were waiting. The amount of goods they had purchased seemed considerable but then Bella had no experience with feeding a family. But maybe it was a good sign.

"Our wives are very industrious women. They grow a lot of stuff and we always have plenty to take into town to sell at the store. They make the best butter too. They also keep hens and collect eggs and stuff. Megan and Eileen will be able to help with those chores."

Megan and Eileen didn't seem to hear him, they were focused on the scenery around them. The actual town was very similar to others they had been to. There was a boardwalk on the main street which comprised of a mercantile, a saloon, and, almost at the other end of town, a church which doubled as a school house. There was also a timber mill and what looked like a blacksmith.

Carl traveled in the wagon with Joe Maitland leaving Bella to travel with Jack. She quickly climbed into the back of the wagon to sit with the girls rather than share the seat with the stranger. He didn't comment on her actions, for which she was thankful.

It took at least thirty minutes to reach the first farmhouse making Bella wonder how the girls would get to school. She knew children walked long distances in the country, but they were only six. She didn't say a word though. It was Carl's job to assess the suitability of the family and while she would air her thoughts to

Bridget, she didn't feel as comfortable sharing them with Carl.

A woman came out to meet them, her gleaming white apron suggesting she had been expecting them. Or maybe she heard them drive up.

"This is my wife, Alice," Jack Maitland said as he stepped down from the wagon. He offered Bella his hand to help her. She accepted, it would have been rude not to. Then she helped both girls down.

"Alice, this is Mr. Carl Watson from the Outplacement Society. This lady is Bella, his assistant. The twin girls are Megan and Eileen, aren't they just adorable?"

Alice nodded in greeting before moving toward the girls who hung back from her, hands held tightly together as usual, the other hands in their respective mouths.

"Are you hungry? Would you like a cookie?" she asked them.

The girls nodded.

"Megan, Eileen, mind your manners. Please say 'yes, please,'" Bella told them.

"Aw, leave them be. Must be hard for them," Alice said, her eyes not leaving the girls.

Bella caught Carl's smile of approval. He seemed to be impressed with Alice.

"Why don't we all go into the house? I have coffee for the adults and milk for the young 'uns."

"Where is your son?" Bella asked, causing Alice to exchange a swift look with her husband.

"Matt and his cousin Barry are up in the field. One of our calves escaped again this morning so they went to catch her. Susan, our girl, is inside. She just woke up. She hasn't been feeling herself today." Alice didn't once meet her eyes. Bella couldn't help but wonder why.

Carl had already gone inside so Bella and the girls followed. Susan, who seemed to be about ten years old, was setting cups on the table. She smiled nervously at Bella but didn't look at her father.

"Good girl, Susan, thank you. This is Megan and her sister Eileen. Can you get them a glass of milk?" Alice asked the girl.

"Yes, Ma," the girl said so quietly Kathleen had to strain to hear her.

"She's a real quiet girl, our Susan. The teacher says she's an angel at school," Alice said as everyone sat.

"Alice bakes the best cookies," Joe said, taking one from the pile. "But don't you go telling my missus. It will only hurt her feelings."

Everyone smiled.

Bella looked around the house, which was clean and very tidy. It didn't look much like a family home. Apart from it being clean, it didn't look like a woman lived there. There were no plants inside nor any works of crochet or knitting. Everything was rather spartan, but then she didn't have much experience with people's houses. She had seen inside Lily's once, but she couldn't compare a red brick New York property to a farmhouse. There was a ladder at the far end of the room which seemed to lead to the loft. Was that where the children slept? As if reading her thoughts, Mrs. Maitland suggested the girls go upstairs.

"Susan, why don't you show the twins where you sleep?" Alice suggested, looking toward the ladder. The girl moved forward without a word. She really was a quiet little thing. There was another door leading to what Bella suspected was the couple's bedroom. A red check curtain partitioned off what she assumed was the cooking area with a back door leading to the outhouse. She wondered where the boy slept. Was it in the loft with his sister? There didn't seem to be a huge space up there, but she didn't want to appear rude by asking.

CHAPTER 29

BELLA

"*B*ella, it is very pretty upstairs. It doesn't look like anyone ever touched the white blankets, they are so clean," Megan said excitedly when she came back downstairs. "There is a doll there too. We weren't allowed to touch it, but I didn't care. We have the dolls you made us." Megan held her rag doll close.

Maybe Susan didn't like to share which would explain why the twins couldn't touch the doll. Bella tried to feel better listening to

Megan's descriptions, but her feelings of un-ease didn't go away.

Mrs. Maitland suggested the children go out and play while the adults talked. Megan was reluctant to leave Bella's side. Bella was caught between going outside with them and staying behind to listen to whatever decisions were made. She opted for the latter, telling Megan she would be out to check on her in a few minutes.

"The girl seems very attached to you, Miss Bella," Jack said.

"Bella was a godsend on the trip down here. She works very well with the children," Carl said. "The twins only recently left home, their father is still alive but not in a position to care for them."

"Will they be allowed to write to their father?" Bella asked, thinking that would be a good way to keep an eye on the girls.

"At six years of age? I wouldn't think they would be able, would they?" Alice asked.

Bella flushed. She had forgotten how

young the twins were. "Well, maybe you could write the letter for them?"

"Alice could, but it might be easier for them to cut the ties now. You know when a calf leaves its mother. It is best done quick." Jack looked at Carl as he spoke.

The children weren't animals, but Bella knew what the man meant. And he was probably right.

"Will Rebecca be joining us?" she asked.

"No, she isn't feeling well today. She sent the boy over to tell us to go ahead and she would see Joe later. I gather there is some paperwork we have to sign? We will agree to send the girls to school and to treat them like our own. I am just sorry we need to split them up," Jack said.

"We understand times are difficult. We are grateful to find such loving homes. They are lovely girls," Carl said, looking quite pleased.

Bella couldn't bear any more. She mumbled an excuse about going to check on the children. When she left the house behind, she couldn't shake the feeling there was something wrong. The Maitland's seemed fine but there was just... she didn't know what it was.

Megan and Eileen were playing catch, but Susan was just sitting watching them.

"Did you not feel like joining in?" Bella asked gently.

The girl flew to her feet. "I was playing, honest. I just wanted to sit for a minute."

"That's fine. It's hot out today. The girls have been cooped up on a train and need some fresh air. Why don't you sit back down and tell me a little about yourself?"

"Me? What do you want to know?" Susan asked suspiciously, her eyes darting to the house.

"How do you feel about getting a new sister?" Bella asked.

"Another pair of hands. Some company to keep them busy." The girl spoke so quietly, Bella had to lean forward to hear her.

"You mean to keep you occupied?" Bella queried.

"Yeah, that's what I meant. I can't sit here talking to you, they won't like it." Susan stood and walked toward the barn. She looked behind as if to check that no one was following her. Bella was tempted to go with her, but at that moment Carl came out of the house accompanied by the other adults.

"Megan, Eileen, these lovely people have asked for you to live with them," Carl said softly but firmly. "We shall be back to see you in about six months' time."

Bella couldn't bear to look at the young girls, Eileen's face crumpled as she burst into tears. Megan stared at Carl in shock.

"I don't think that is wise, is it? They will have just settled in," Jack Maitland said. "We don't want to upset the children."

Carl faced Jack.

"No, of course we don't, but it has always been the rule of the society to check."

"Really? I haven't heard of anyone coming to Mud Butte unless they had a load of orphans with them," Jack said.

"I'm afraid things didn't always work like they should have, but from now on it will be different," Carl said firmly. "It is to protect both the children and the people offering them homes. We hope the placements work out well, but sometimes it is necessary to remove the children. By checking up on each placement we hope to avoid any issues."

Bella saw Joe and Jack exchange a quick glance, but Carl seemed to miss it. He had bent down to say goodbye to the twins. "So, girls, we will see you in October. Be good for the Maitlands."

Megan ran from Carl to Bella, holding her dress.

"Bella, please don't leave us," Megan begged. "We don't want to live in different houses."

Bella couldn't let the girls see how upset she was, that wouldn't be fair. Thankfully, she was an expert at hiding her emotions.

"Megan, we knew the reason you were on the train was to find you new homes. We can't find one for both of you, so this is the best alternative."

She gave each of the twins a hug and told them they would be happy with their new parents. "This way you both get to see one another. You will be going to the same school, church, and everything."

She gave them another quick hug and walked quickly to the wagon. Jack Maitland had offered to drive herself and Carl back to town. She would prefer to have walked back to town rather than sit near to Jack Maitland, but Carl thanked him kindly saying he wanted to get back to his wife. She assumed Joe would take Eileen to his house as Alice appeared to have taken a liking to Megan. She wished, with every beat of her heart, Kathleen was with her. She could have spoken to the other girl about her fears. Maybe Carl and Bridget would have listened to Bridget's sister.

CHAPTER 30

KATHLEEN

Kathleen fidgeted in her seat. She couldn't concentrate on her book and she was sick of looking at the scenery. One field looked pretty much like another from the train. A couple of days passed by, the train moving slowly as one issue after another seemed to plague it. There weren't any more fires thank goodness, but a rail had been bent and they had run out of water. If she was superstitious she would think something was trying to prevent her from reaching Cedar Falls.

"Where are you going?" Miss Screed asked as Kathleen stood.

"To check on Patrick. I haven't seen him yet today."

The woman gave her a knowing look, "To throw yourself at the handsome doctor more like. I know what you Irish girls are like. But he won't be interested in the likes of you. He needs a well brought up young lady. Used to the ways of his type."

"I have no intention of throwing myself at anyone, Miss Screed. I assure you I was brought up properly. I wish to check on Patrick. That is all," Kathleen replied coldly before sweeping out of the car. She gripped her hands so hard, her nails made marks in her flesh. She hated that woman with a passion. She was going to see Patrick, not the doctor. The poor boy would be lonely. Miss Screed was wrong. She had no interest in Doctor Richard. He was too old for her for a start as well as being rich and part of the upper class.

Was it her imagination or did his eyes

widen with pleasure when he saw her at the door of the car.

"Come in, Miss Collins, we were just wondering when you would visit us, weren't we, Patrick?"

Patrick seemed rather sleepy.

"I had to give him some laudanum for the pain. He may sleep."

"Poor Patrick. I hope you feel better. I best get back to the others," she replied, turning back toward the door.

"Why don't you sit down and have some tea. I am being selfish, I find train journeys so boring. It helps to pass the time."

She took a seat, careful to keep her distance. He poured some tea and handed it to her with a selection of cookies.

"The nice ones are gone. Patrick likes the chocolate ones," he apologized.

"This is lovely, thank you," Kathleen replied.

"How did you find yourself on this train, Miss Collins?" Dr. Richard asked. "Forgive me for asking, but my curiosity is getting the better of me. You are not looking for a placement and you're a little young to be an employee of the agency."

She hesitated, wondering if he would think she was on a wild-goose chase.

"I am looking for my brothers. They were sent west on an orphan train last year and we haven't heard from them since. A friend of the family, Father Nelson, works closely with the Children's Aid Society and introduced me to Mr. Loring Brace. He agreed to let me come with this group of orphans. In return for my help with the children, he paid my fare."

"Oh, I am sorry," he said. "Why was your family separated?"

She hesitated which he mistook for her being insulted.

"I apologize. I shouldn't have asked. It is none of my business," he went on hastily.

"No, don't be sorry. I don't have anything to hide. I have three sisters and three brothers. Liam and Annie, the younger two, were adopted by a couple, Mr. and Mrs. Rees, who live in Wyoming. My sister, Bridget, who accompanied them to Wyoming, met and married the outplacement agent. My brothers, Shane and Michael, didn't go on the same train as Bridget. We believe they went to Iowa."

"And you? You didn't want to head West?"

Kathleen shook her head, keeping her eyes down. She didn't want to admit to having been afraid of moving outside of New York.

"I live and work at a women's sanctuary in New York and have been saving for the cost of the ticket to try to find my brothers. When Father Nelson suggested I accompany Miss Screed as a helper, it meant I could come sooner than planned. But I plan on returning to New York." Something stopped her from mentioning her plans to go to Riverside Springs.

Richard didn't say anything for the next few seconds. Had she been too forthcoming about her family? Maybe he was wondering how to get away from her without being rude? She was about to stand and give the excuse he needed by telling him she should go check on the orphans.

"I am so sorry your family were separated," he said before she could make her excuses. "What happened to your other sister?"

"My other sister?"

"You said you had three. But you only spoke about Bridget and Annie."

Kathleen looked away from his face. Wishing she had never said anything about her family, she tried to find the best words to describe the situation.

"Maura, she's the eldest. She decided to take a job elsewhere. We are estranged." Kathleen didn't like lying but she wasn't about to tell the doctor her sister had stolen from Lily and run away. She stood quickly. "I best check on Josie and the others. They might be running rings around Miss Screed."

CHAPTER 31

BELLA

*B*ella didn't hear a word of Jack and Carl's conversation as they made their way back to Mud Butte. She couldn't help wondering why Susan looked so uncomfortable in her own home. She was glad when they reached the hotel, hoping to talk to Bridget about her concerns. But her friend was still ill. She considered speaking to Carl, but he kept saying how nice the Maitlands were, so she didn't think he would listen to her. She went to her room early, claiming tiredness, but didn't sleep a wink all night. The next morning, she hoped Bridget would be up to talking but instead Carl had called the doctor. He was so worried about his wife, Bella couldn't burden him with her concerns. Especially as they were simply her feelings. She had no evidence of any wrongdoing.

TWO DAYS after leaving the children, she made her way to the mercantile, hoping she might meet the owner's wife. Given the amount of goods the Maitlands had, the owner was bound to know them. Even better, she might bump into the family out shopping.

But when she walked inside there was no sign of a female assistant. She couldn't bring herself to ask the hard-faced man behind the counter any questions. He would probably assume she was gossiping as all men seemed to when a woman asked questions. She bought a cent's worth of candy for Bridget and left quickly.

As she left, she almost walked into a lady who was coming in. The lady stopped and smiled in greeting. Bella returned the smile and was about to walk away when the woman spoke.

"Forgive me, you probably don't remember me, but I was wondering if you found a home for the twin girls. My name is Gracie…"

"MacDonagh. You were there with your husband." Bella's heart beat faster. She had liked this couple and had hoped they would decide to take the twins. She wondered if she knew the Maitlands, but before she could ask, Sheriff Slater approached the store, nodding to them. Was it her imagination, or did Gracie MacDonagh stiffen beside her? She didn't blame Gracie. The sheriff gave her the creeps. It wasn't his whiskers or beard, although she wasn't keen on facial hair. It was his eyes, they were utterly devoid of feeling. Cold and almost black, they sent shivers down her back and it wasn't pleasant.

"Morning, ladies. Fine day, isn't it?" He

turned his gaze to Bella who immediately felt guilty, although she had done nothing wrong. "I thought you would be long gone by now. Seeing as you found homes for all those children."

"Yes, sir, we did, but Mrs. Watson fell ill. She should be ready to continue our journey to Riverside Springs tomorrow."

"I am sorry to hear that," he said. "Please pass on my best wishes. I am sure you folks are keen to get on with your journey."

Bella nodded. She wasn't comfortable with lawmen, or anyone in authority if she was honest. The family who'd taken her in years before had been seen as pillars of their community. When she had run to the local sheriff for help, he had packed her back home with a clip around her ear, telling her she should be grateful a decent family had provided a vagrant like her with a good home.

"Is that the time? Giles will be wondering where I am. Good day, Sheriff." Mrs. Mac-Donagh nodded in Bella's direction and was gone before she could offer to walk with her. The Sheriff continued to stare at her.

"I best be getting back to the Watsons," she mumbled before turning on her heel and heading toward the hotel. Thankful he didn't follow her, she risked a glance back at the mercantile to find him still staring after her. She quickened her step and walked straight into Carl.

"Bella, good grief, are you all right? You're shaking."

"I'm fine," Bella told him. "How is Bridget?"

"Better now, thank you. We will be able to leave tomorrow."

"Good. I don't like this town."

Carl gave her a funny look but didn't say anything. Bella made some excuse about packing and walked quickly to her room. Once the door closed, she let the tears come. Frustration and rage battled with sadness. Why did any child have to go and live with strangers? It just wasn't right.

CHAPTER 32

BELLA

The next morning, Bridget arrived down to breakfast looking very pale.

"Maybe you should rest more," Bella suggested. "You don't look well enough to travel."

"I am fine, thank you," Bridget said, offering her a smile. "How are you? Are you missing the children?"

Bella nodded.

"I think it was very brave of you to travel with us and help with the orphans. You grew very close to the twins and I understand it was difficult letting them go. I know with your experiences, it must have brought back some horrible memories. I hope you don't let your past prevent you from having a good future."

Bella didn't say anything. She couldn't burden Bridget with her worries, and maybe Bridget was right. She was letting her past overshadow everything.

"Tomorrow, we'll travel by train to Green River where we'll catch a stage coach to Riverside Springs."

"I bet you're excited about seeing Liam and Annie again," Bella said, more for something to say. She knew Bridget would worry if she didn't talk.

"Yes, I am. But I am a little nervous too. I don't want to upset them at their new home."

"I am sure they will be delighted to see you, Bridget."

* * *

THEY ARRIVED in Riverside Springs to the sounds of screams of excitement as two young children nearly knocked them over in their haste to greet them.

"Sorry, Bridget, but they have been waiting for days for you to arrive."

Bella stood back to let the family reunite. Both Liam and Annie had blossomed in the year since leaving New York. They were not only taller and healthier-looking, but their happiness was evident. She closed her eyes, hoping the same would prove true for all the other children on the train.

"Geoff and Carolyn, this is Bella Jones," Bridget said, gesturing toward her.

"Pleased to meet you, Miss Jones," Carolyn said, shaking her hand. "I hope you find Riverside Springs to your liking. Bridget wrote to tell us you were a talented seamstress. I look forward to buying a new dress."

"One dress? Now that is something I have to see," Geoff Rees commented, she could see he was teasing by the loving look he sent his wife. "Nice to meet you, Miss Jones." He tipped his hat to her.

A tall thin man with brown hair and lovely eyes shining with kindness came to join them. He was accompanied by a dog who wagged his tail in greeting when Bella bent down to pat his head. Bella looked up in time to catch the man's eye and couldn't look away. It was as if she was drawn to him. His eyes widened as he stared back at her. A couple of seconds passed before she broke eye contact, but when she stole another glance, he was still staring at her. Oddly, his appraisal didn't make her uncomfortable.

"This is Brian Curran," Bridget said. "He and Mitch over here were orphan train children too, years and years ago. And this is Shannon, Mitch's wife."

"It is so nice to have another woman in town, Miss Jones," Shannon said with a welcoming smile.

"Please, call me Bella. I have heard so much about everyone I feel like I know you all," Bella said.

Mitch shook her hand then Brian's. She almost snatched hers away as he held it, the shivers ran up her arm. He seemed to feel something too, if the color on his face was anything to go by.

Flustered, she turned to greet the children. "You both have grown up so fast, I wouldn't recognize you."

"I look like Bridget, that's what Ma says," Annie mentioned, casting a glance at Carolyn.

"You do indeed, Annie," the woman said, beaming.

"Ma says you will make me a new dress too," Annie said to her.

"I would love to do that," Bella said.

"But first, I'm certain she would like a cup of tea and a sit down after that stage journey" an older woman said firmly. It could only be Mrs. Grayson.

CHAPTER 33

BELLA

"I'm Mrs. Grayson," the older woman said, confirming Bella's suspicions. "Come along now, everyone, let's go inside out of the heat."

Bella followed Bridget and the rest inside, smiling at how Mrs. Grayson lived up to Bridget's description. She was glad to sit down on a chair that didn't move, although, she really would have preferred to sleep for the next forty-eight hours.

"I will show you the shop and the room

you can use for your new venture after you've had some refreshments."

"Thank you, Mrs. Grayson," Bella said. "I am really grateful to you."

"Bella, is it okay if I call you that? We are a lot less formal than your city folk. I'm glad you're here and I'm looking forward to selling lots more thread, fabrics, and hats. Business will boom. I have your room ready too. You can share with Kathleen when she arrives. I assume that's agreeable to both of you."

Bella nodded.

"When will Kathleen be joining us, Bridget?" Mrs. Grayson asked.

"I am not sure, probably in a couple of months. I will explain why later," Bridget responded.

"She means when we're not here to listen," Liam piped up, making everyone laugh.

"Now, Liam Rees, don't be rude," Mrs. Grayson admonished the child before handing him another cookie. "Why don't you take

Annie out for a run around and let us talk in peace."

"Sure." Liam grabbed the cookies and was gone with Annie hot on his heels.

"Such sweet children," Mrs. Grayson said as they left.

"Mrs. Grayson is like the children's grandmother and Brian their uncle," Carolyn Rees explained to Bella. Looking up, she caught Brian's eye again, this time noting his crimson cheeks. He was shy.

"Mrs. Rees, would you mind if we went home now? Bridget hasn't been feeling well," Carl asked quietly.

"Of course, I am so sorry. We shall go immediately. Bella, would you like to join us? You could share Annie's room?" Carolyn Rees suggested.

"No, thank you," Bella said, despite wanting to stay with Bridget and people she knew. She had to stand on her own feet sometime. It might as well start now. Mrs. Grayson smiled her approval.

"Bridget, you rest," Mrs. Grayson said. "I'll look after Bella here and, between myself and Shannon, we will introduce her to plenty of new customers."

"I'll be back in town in a couple of days, so I'll talk to you about my dress then," Carolyn said before calling the children to tell them they were going home.

Bella waved off the family then returned to the store.

"You look dead on your feet, young lady," Mrs. Grayson said, eyeing her up and down. "Why don't you go and lie down for a while? Tomorrow will be here soon enough."

"I wouldn't like you to think I was taking advantage," Bella protested.

"I insist," Mrs. Grayson said, her tone telling Bella to obey.

Bella accepted, grateful to put her head down. She hoped her mind would switch off and let her sleep.

The room was very pretty with a beautiful quilt on the bed, matching the drapes on the window. The floor was polished to a high shine. There was a jug and basin on the washstand with some hooks for her dresses and a chest of drawers for her other things.

She undressed and slipped beneath the covers, but sleep eluded her. She couldn't help but think of the twins and wonder what they were doing. Could she discuss her fears with Mrs. Grayson? Probably not a good idea. She could already tell the woman had a good heart, but she didn't want to get off on the wrong foot. Anything bad she said about the orphan trains could be interpreted as a criticism of the work Carl and Bridget did. Oh, why did Bridget have to be ill? Bella was sure if Bridget had been out at the farm she would have had second thoughts of leaving the twins there. If Kathleen was with her, she could talk to her, but her friend was somewhere in Iowa. She wondered if she had found her missing brothers yet.

CHAPTER 34

KATHLEEN

Kathleen finally had her first breakthrough. Their train had stopped to take on coal and water and she had volunteered to walk to the store to get some provisions for their journey. On her way, she had called into the church. Her mam used to tell her the priest knew everyone in a town. She assumed the same would hold true for a pastor or reverend.

As luck would have it, the pastor remembered meeting her brothers. He said they had moved onto the next town and he had heard they were living on a farm near a town called Freesburg. The pastor promised to telegram the priest in Freesburg requesting he set up a meeting, if possible, with her brothers.

She skipped back to the train, her heart bursting with joy, she couldn't wait to put her arms around them both, especially Shane. They had always been close. Her earliest memory was sitting on the steps of the tenements chatting to Shane, they must have been about five and six years old. She met Doctor Richard at the train. "Miss Collins, you look very happy. Would you care to take a walk with me and tell me why? The children are with Miss Screed including Patrick."

She was torn between checking on Patrick and going for the walk. She chose the latter, she had to tell someone about her brothers or she would burst. As they walked, she told him of her meeting with the priest and the information he had given her.

"What are your plans after you see your brothers?" Dr. Richard asked her.

She took a deep breath. Could she really admit she was hoping they would return to New York with her then move out to Riverside Springs? Would he think she was naïve? She didn't even know the terms of their placements. Some boys were indentured until age twenty-one, which would mean her brothers could be stuck in Iowa for the next few years. Even if she could convince them to return to New York, what then? Would they come to Riverside Springs? Would there be jobs for them? All these questions.

"I shall return to New York, and from there I will move to Riverside Springs in Wyoming. I hope that my brothers accompany me. I would love my family to be back together. That's my dream." She shifted from one foot to another.

"What's so special about Riverside Springs? I never heard of it."

"It's a small but growing town. A nice community or so my sisters tell me. My younger siblings were adopted by a family living near there. My sister Bridget and her husband use the town as their base when they're not working on the trains."

"I see," he said. "What shall you do in this Riverside Springs?"

He wasn't laughing at her. He didn't seem to think her dream was ridiculous. If anything, he seemed genuinely interested in what she had to say. She blushed at his scrutiny.

"I want to have my own dressmaking shop," Bridget told him, lowering her voice to almost a whisper. She didn't want anyone laughing at her ambitions which probably sounded a bit silly to a doctor. "My friend, Bella Jones, went ahead of me and she is going to start a dressmaking service. When I get there, we hope to have enough customers to have our own business."

"I love how ambitious you are, Miss

Collins. So many ladies are content just to be a pretty face."

She blushed at him calling her pretty, aware he wasn't being condescending. He looked like he meant every word. For someone she had just met, his opinion of her meant a great deal. Perhaps too much. Kathleen Collins, you need to be careful or Miss Screed will be proved right. He is a doctor and from a totally different class to you. But despite the inner voice in her head, she couldn't help but be thrilled he thought her pretty.

"Where will you leave the train, Doctor?" she asked.

"I was planning on going to Waterloo, but now I think I shall get off in Freesburg. If you have no objection, I would like to see you get to meet your brothers. But I also have an ulterior motive. I want to make sure Patrick's hands are completely healed and there is a wonderful doctor in Freesburg. As it happens," he added.

"That is rather coincidental, isn't it?" she

said, half-teasing him. She felt at ease with him despite only knowing him a short time. The age gap didn't seem to matter. His eyes glowed as he realized she had caught him out.

"It is, I suppose," he said before smiling. His smile made his eyes crinkle up. She could tell he smiled and laughed a lot.

"How will you get Miss Screed to allow you to keep Patrick with you?" she asked, her curiosity getting the better of her. Miss Screed had insisted the children had to be taken in by families. Single men were not allowed to adopt, and certainly not single women.

"Money talks, Miss Collins, surely you have learnt that by now?" his tone was more sarcastic than he had ever used before.

She stared at him, horrified at what he had said.

"You can't mean to buy him?" She didn't hide her shock.

"Of course, I won't buy him. Not in the traditional sense. But in return for a substantial donation, I believe Miss Screed will sign the paperwork."

"What do you plan to do with him?" Kathleen couldn't believe it would be that easy, but then again, money did make life a lot easier. She wasn't at all sure she approved.

"I mentioned I think he has a wonderful mind. I would like to help him get adopted but by the correct family. I think, with the right education, our young friend can achieve great things."

"But you're single?" Blushing, she put a hand up to her mouth. "Forgive me."

She couldn't believe she had told him she had thought about his marital state. How awkward could she be? She closed her eyes imagining Shane beside her. Her brother would have laughed his head off at her clumsiness.

"I wasn't clear in my intentions. I have some good friends whose children have grown up. I know they will take great care of Patrick. They are currently out of the country but, on their return, I am sure they will grow as fond of him as I have."

"And if they don't?" Kathleen didn't want to believe that would happen, but she didn't want Patrick to get hurt either. He had been through enough rejection already.

"Then I will keep him." He sounded so sure of himself. Was this what having money and privilege gave you? Supreme confidence in your ability to do anything you wanted.

He looked at her carefully as if reading her thoughts. She looked away.

"Shall we return to the train and see what Patrick thinks?"

When they told him the doctor's plans, Patrick was thrilled he'd be staying with them for a while longer. Kathleen knew the boy wanted Richard to adopt him. He had barely left the doctor's side since they first met. She thought Richard felt the same, but it wasn't yet acceptable for a single man to adopt.

"Don't frown so much. Things have a way of working out," Richard whispered to her, making her laugh. Being around him, she could believe that. Then she remembered the reality. When you came from the tenements of New York it was hard to believe things would work out.

CHAPTER 35

BELLA

The next morning, Bella woke late. She couldn't believe the sun was high in the sky. Dressing quickly, she came downstairs to find Mrs. Grayson baking. The smell of cinnamon made her stomach grumble loudly.

"Good morning." Mrs. Grayson greeted her with a smile.

"I am so sorry, I didn't mean to oversleep. What can I do?" Bella pushed her sleeves up.

"Sit down and have a cup of coffee. What

would you like for breakfast? I can make some flapjacks if you're hungry?"

"But I am so late," Bella protested.

"Bella, you have only just arrived after a very tiring journey. I know from Bridget's letters you are a hard worker. So, please, relax."

Bella couldn't believe her ears. The woman was so kind, yet she barely knew her. She took a seat as the woman fussed around her.

"To be honest, I love having someone here to chat with. My husband, well he's a man and given to few words. So, what do you think of Riverside Springs? I know you've only just arrived, but does it look like somewhere you could live?"

"Yes, Mrs. Grayson."

"I'll show you the work room in a bit. It used to be a store room, but we didn't really use it. When I heard you were coming, I cleared it out and paid Brian Curran to put in some windows. He's just finishing it up now."

Bella's head jerked up. "Mr. Curran is here?"

"Yes, he's been out there since the crack of dawn. He was anxious to get it finished," Mrs. Grayson explained.

"Everyone has been so kind," Bella said, still finding it hard to believe.

"We want you to stay here," Mrs. Grayson said. "Riverside Springs needs new people to make it grow into a bigger town. We know a railway station would help, but until we get more people living here, the railway won't come out this far. So, we are being selfish really. Now eat up."

Bella tucked into the stack of flapjacks. She was so glad Kathleen had talked her into making this trip. Ignoring her misgivings about the twins, everything else was working out so well.

When she was finished she insisted on doing the washing up. Mrs. Grayson dried the dishes and together they worked well.

"Now, let's take young Brian out some lunch and coffee. You can see the space available and how you might want to organize it. Mr. Rees also has a present for you."

"A present for me? But why?" Bella asked.

"It was for Kathleen originally, but he said you are to use it and when she comes he will get her another one," Mrs. Grayson said.

Intrigued, Bella followed the woman out to the store room. It was a big bright space thanks in part to the two new windows. Brian nodded his head in greeting, unable to speak as his mouth was full of nails.

She walked around the room, her fingers trailing along the table as she came to the sewing machine.

"It's new," she marveled.

"Yes, hasn't been used," Mrs. Grayson said. "Have you used one before?"

"Yes, in the sanctuary. Mrs. Grayson, this is all wonderful," Bella gushed, before hugging the older woman. She sprang back just as quickly. "Sorry, I don't know what came over me."

"I do," Mrs. Grayson said. "It was excitement and it's lovely to see. I can't wait for you to start sewing. My mother used to say I stood behind the door when God was giving out sewing talent. I can get by, but it will be so nice to have a professional here."

"I will make you the first dress," Bella promised. "Tell me what fabric you like, and we can start today."

"Not today, Bella," Mrs. Grayson said. "Brian is going to put up a rail over there, so you can hang a drape. That way, your customers can try on the garments you make. And over here, we thought you could store the fabrics in such a way as to tempt people into making new purchases."

"You've thought of everything," Bella said excitedly, wanting to pinch herself to check she wasn't dreaming.

"You can change things around if you want to. You are in charge."

Bella couldn't believe it. After all these years, she had finally found someone who seemed to think her worthy of something. To be fair, Lily had been the first person to treat her like a human being, but Mrs. Grayson seemed to believe she could do anything.

"Thank you," she said, suddenly shy. What if she didn't live up to expectations? What if the woman found out about her past?

"Don't thank me when you're working twelve hours a day trying to keep up with demand." Mrs. Grayson laughed then wiggled her nose. "Oh, my goodness, I think I forgot to take the beans off the cooker. I'll be back in a minute."

The woman moved fast for an older person. Bella was conscious she and Brian were alone now. Not that it wasn't proper, the door was wide open, and anyone could come in.

"Thank you, Mr. Curran, for doing this," she said.

He took the nails from his mouth. "No need for thanks. I'm glad you decided to come here, I mean, we're all glad you came." Brian's words trailed off as his cheeks turned bright red. She smiled but that seemed to make him even more embarrassed.

"I best go inside," she said, turning to leave.

"Miss Jones, when you have time later, maybe tomorrow evening, would you like to go for a walk? I could show you around the town," Brian suggested.

Bella pretended to be examining the sewing machine. Could she go for a walk with a man? What if he thought it might lead to something? It wasn't fair to pretend to be something she wasn't. But all he'd asked was for her to take a walk. He was probably just being friendly.

"I can ask Mrs. Grayson to come with us if you feel the need for a chaperone?" he said.

She shook her head. "A walk sounds nice. Thank you."

CHAPTER 36

BELLA

The next morning Bridget and Carl called to the Mercantile. Mrs Grayson escorted them into the kitchen calling Bella to come see her visitors. Bella came downstairs, relieved to see that Bridget was looking better than she had the day before.

"Kathleen sent me a telegram," Bridget said. "She's on her way to Iowa to find our brothers. I didn't want to say anything in front of Liam or Annie."

"I can understand, you might get their hopes up," Mrs. Grayson said.

"How are things here?" Bridget asked, looking at Bella. But before she could answer, Mrs. Grayson spoke up.

"Bella has settled in just lovely, haven't you dear? She can show you her workshop in a minute. Brian Curran has been fixing it up for her." Mrs. Grayson elbowed Bella gently. "I think he may have fallen for our new arrival already."

Bella's face heated up as she wished she could be anywhere but sitting at the table. Bridget smiled, a satisfied look on her face. Bella knew Bridget had originally come to Riverside Springs to marry Brian, but it was obvious her friend had no romantic feelings for him. Bridget was madly in love with her husband Carl. When Carl asked Mrs. Grayson for something in the store, the two of them left, leaving Bella and Bridget alone.

"Mrs. Grayson means well. She wouldn't want to embarrass you," Bridget said softly.

"I know. It's just awkward being the center

of attention. I feel everyone is looking at me and…"

"And what?"

"Waiting for me to make a mess of things," Bella said, feeling miserable.

"Bella, when will you believe in yourself? We all do. Nobody in Riverside Springs thinks you'll make a mess of things. On the contrary, everyone is impressed by how hard you have already been working helping Mrs. Grayson in the store as well as getting things ready for the dress shop. You seem to have settled in very well. Let this fresh start be your chance to put the past behind you."

"But," Bella looked around to make sure Mrs. Grayson hadn't returned, "you know I can't let a man have a real interest in me. It wouldn't be fair."

"Why not?" Bridget asked. "You're a lovely woman and Brian is a wonderful man."

"He won't want me, not when he knows about me."

"Bella, he will want the person you are becoming. A woman who cares about others, who fights for their welfare. You fought for Annie and you fought for the twins. Someone without a loving heart wouldn't have done that. Stop being so hard on yourself." Bridget placed her hand on Bella's. "I wish we could stay longer and see you settled in properly, but we have to return to New York."

"So soon?" Bella couldn't stop herself from saying.

"Yes. Carl is insisting I see someone. Please don't tell the others, but he's concerned about me. My dizzy spells are getting worse. I told him we could go to the doctor here. I'm not even sure there is one, but he insists on going home."

"Bridget, you must do as he says. We need you to get better. The children need you. So do I."

"Thank you, Bella. I'm sure I'll be fine. Do me a favor though and give yourself and Brian a chance. He asked me to find him a wife. Maybe that's one promise I got to keep."

Bridget's eyes danced telling Bella her friend was teasing her, but a wife? Was that how Brian saw her?

"Bridget are you ready to go and say goodbye to the others?" Carl walked back into the room closely followed by Mrs. Grayson.

"Goodbye? Don't tell me you're leaving already," Mrs. Grayson said, looking put out. "I thought you would stay and visit with us for a while."

"I would love to, but duty calls," Bridget said, winking at Bella. "There are more orphans in New York and the agency is short of placement agents. We'll come out here again soon."

"We will look after Bella while you're gone," Mrs. Grayson promised. "Don't wait too long to come back. We miss you, Bridget."

Bella saw the telling sparkle in Bridget's eyes, so she distracted Mrs. Grayson by asking her about using the catalogue. The older woman explained it was used to buy items that were too big to store in the mercantile. While

Mrs. Grayson spoke, Bridget blew her a grateful kiss and was gone before Mrs. Grayson realized. Bella hoped Bridget would be able to find a doctor to cure her. She didn't want to think about losing her friend.

CHAPTER 37

BELLA

The rest of the day passed in a whirlwind as Mrs. Grayson brought more women to the store, introducing them to Bella and outlining her talents. Bella almost wished she could cancel the walk with Brian and get to work on the dresses right away. Almost.

She changed into her other dress, the one she kept for Sundays at the sanctuary. She patted some of her precious rose water onto her wrists. Lily had given her the bottle when she left, in addition to a small sum of money. She had written her a lovely note, too, saying how much she would miss Bella and what a wonderful young woman she was becoming.

She wondered what Lily would think of her agreeing to go for a walk with Brian Curran. She had only just arrived in town. Would people think she was fast?

She walked down the stairs to find Mrs. Grayson in the sitting room, her knitting on her lap.

"Don't you scrub up well," the woman said, appraising her. "That dress is very becoming."

"Do you think so?" Bella asked, fanning out the skirt. "I made it."

"It's beautiful, dear."

"Kathleen helped me with the design," Bella said. "She's very talented."

"I think you both are," Mrs. Grayson added. "Are you going for a walk with Brian?"

Bella blushed. "Yes. Do you think I shouldn't?"

"I think it's a wonderful idea. He is a fine man. You will be quite safe with him."

"You don't think people will think less of me?" Bella asked quietly.

"Less of you? Why should they? Haven't young men and women been courting since Noah built the ark? It's the most natural thing in the world."

"I only just arrived in town," Bella protested.

"Brian knows he has to be quick. There are very few single women out here, Bella. You'll soon find a trail of admirers at your door."

Bella shuddered. The last thing she wanted was men coming after her.

"Bella, stop thinking and just enjoy yourself," Mrs. Grayson ordered. "Brian Curran is a man I would trust with my own daughter. Go on, have a little fun. Life is hard enough without missing out on simple pleasures."

"Thank you, Mrs. Grayson."

Brian knocked on the door. When she opened it, he had a small posy of flowers in his hand. "I picked them for you,' he said, almost throwing them at her.

She heard Mrs. Grayson laugh but the old woman quickly turned it into a cough. It looked like she wasn't the only one nervous about the walk.

CHAPTER 38

BELLA

"Why don't we walk along the river?" Brian suggested once they were outside. "I always find the sound of water to be soothing."

Bella nodded but she had no real experience of walking beside any water. She hadn't time in New York and where she had lived before... She closed her mind to those memories.

As they walked, they talked about various things, including her plans for the dress shop, and her hopes Kathleen would join her in Riverside Springs. Brian was easy to talk to.

He asked questions without making her feel like he was interrogating her.

He spoke a little about himself and his farm which he was rebuilding after losing cattle to rustlers the year before. He told her about Mitch and Shannon and how much they were looking forward to the arrival of their first baby.

She told him about Kathleen, wondering aloud whether she had found her brothers. Brian knew about Bridget's family.

"Miss Jones, I guess you know I was supposed to marry Bridget," he said, his ears and neck turning crimson. He stared into the river. "I had written off for a mail order bride."

"Yes, she told me. I'm sorry it didn't work out for you," she replied stiffly, wondering why he had brought Bridget up. She wasn't a bit like the other woman who was older, stronger, and not to mention, innocent.

"I just wanted you to know that I am glad things didn't work out," he said quietly.

She looked at him before looking back at the river in embarrassment.

Flustered, he blurted out, "Of course she is a wonderful woman, Bridget, I mean, and Carl is very lucky, but she wasn't the right woman for me. That's what I was trying to say."

Bella didn't respond at first. She didn't know what to say.

"Maybe it's time we got back," she suggested after a few moments of awkward silence.

"Oh, now I've scared you off. I am not very good with women. I mean, I don't know how to talk to ladies," Brian said.

Bella stopped walking.

"I like you, Miss Jones. And I would like to get to know you better. I just wanted you to know that."

He took her arm and escorted her back to Grayson's store. When they got there, he took off his hat and nodded.

"Thank you for the walk."

Then he was gone.

CHAPTER 39

BELLA

*T*he week passed by quickly as Bella got set up with her new work space. She made Mrs. Grayson's dress first, as promised. The older woman couldn't believe how well it turned out, making Bella blush with her compliments.

"Even Mr. Grayson noticed, and he never notices anything," Mrs. Grayson told her. "You have such talent, my girl. You are going to do so well with your new business."

Bella beamed with happiness. Carolyn

Rees also called in and ordered two dresses for herself and two for Annie. Annie helped pick out the material, although she had to be guided away from a pale pink to a fresh navy gingham.

"This will be much better for hiding the dirt you seem to pick up wherever you go, darling," Carolyn said to her daughter, putting her arm around her shoulders.

Their obvious closeness made Bella feel lonely. She was rather surprised, as she didn't usually notice the relationships of those around her. But seeing Annie reminded her of Megan and Eileen. She hoped the twins were getting on as well with their respective new mothers.

On Sunday, she went to Reverend Franklins' service with the Graysons. Afterward, Brian invited her to join him at Mitch and Shannon's for dinner. Her hopes rose, thinking he wanted to spend time with her, but his next words proved Shannon to be the one issuing the invitation. She couldn't help but be disappointed.

"Shannon asked me to invite you," Brian said. "She would love some company. With the baby coming, she doesn't get into town and, Mitch, he isn't much for chitchat."

"I will have to check with Mrs. Grayson. She may need me." Bella wasn't keen on spending more time with Brian. She was losing sleep wondering if he liked her then worrying what would happen if he did. Then she'd convince herself he couldn't like someone like her and that made her feel worse. Unfortunately, Mrs. Grayson was right behind her and responded without being asked.

"It's Sunday, Bella. You don't have to work today. Off you go and enjoy yourself."

She couldn't get out of it now without seeming rude. So, Bella decided she might as well make the best of it.

To her surprise, she enjoyed the short ride out to Mitch's place. Brian didn't mention Bridget or anything relating to them. He told her of his friendship with Mitch, how they had met on the orphan train and more or less considered each other family. She didn't volunteer any information about her background, but Brian didn't seem to notice.

CHAPTER 40

BELLA

Shannon was everything Bridget had said, warm and friendly. Her pregnancy had slowed her down a little, but it didn't stop her chattering away nineteen to the dozen. She'd prepared a pot roast with all the trimmings including baked potatoes heaped with mountains of butter. Bella had to stop herself from having seconds. She didn't want to appear greedy in front of the others. Conversation flowed with Shannon and Mitch teasing Brian then Bella. She couldn't believe how natural it seemed for the four of them to carry on a conversation. There were no uncomfortable silences.

After everyone had declared themselves to be full, Mitch asked Brian to check on his horse.

"He has such a way with animals," Shannon said as the two women cleared up. "He can fix up most things."

"He did a lot of work on the area Mrs. Grayson gave me for my workshop. Put in new windows and everything," Bella said, stirring her coffee so she wouldn't have to look at Shannon. She could feel the woman looking at her.

"He made sure to make your workshop a priority. Brian is a good man. He would make an excellent husband and father when the time comes."

Embarrassed, Bella tried changing the subject. "I saw your garden. You seem to have all sorts growing in it."

Shannon chuckled, letting Bella know she

knew she'd changed the topic of conversation, but she didn't change it back.

"My mother taught me everything I know. I was adopted by a Pastor and his wife. They didn't always have much money, so Ma used to make the money we did have stretch further by growing her own stuff. Farming here can be a little tricky, you got to make sure the ground isn't too cold when you plant stuff. Mitch gave me part of the barn to use, so I plant my seeds there first then I transfer them out to the ground in May when it warms up a little. The first frosts come in August, so you have to harvest as much as you can before then. You also have to pick crops that suit our climate. Watermelons do great. I love watermelons."

Bella smiled at the look of pleasure on Shannon's face.

The woman continued. "Lettuces and radishes. Cabbage, peas, and carrots work too. Apples grow themselves. I mean, I don't have to do anything to help them. Strawberries and raspberries too, but I miss other things. When I was little, we lived near Florida and you could grow lemons and oranges."

"I never tasted a lemon. Had an orange a couple of times at Christmas," Bella added.

"Yes, that's what it was like for Mitch and Brian. They tell me I am spoiled," Shannon said.

Bella didn't think Shannon was at all spoiled, but she didn't say so. She wasn't about to contradict her host's husband. She noticed the woman was yawning again.

"Why don't you sit down in that rocking chair and take the weight off your feet for a little bit. I can tidy up." Bella offered.

Although she looked tempted, Shannon protested, "I can't invite you to dinner and expect you to clear up."

"I offered."

"I won't say no," Shannon said, giving in. "To be honest, I feel so big I think I am going to burst. I wish this baby would come already."

Bella watched the woman caress her bump.

"Do you want a girl or a boy?" she

asked her.

"I guess a boy, as that would make Mitch happy. You know how men are with their sons. But, to be honest, I don't mind either way. I just want it born." Shannon smiled but Bella could see she was exhausted.

"Close your eyes, you look tired. I will have these dishes done in no time. And I think I'll take a walk afterward. You live in such a pretty place."

Shannon grinned. "I am the luckiest woman in the world. Mitch does all he can to make things nice for me."

Shannon put her head back on the rocking chair. Bella took the dishes to the sink and, using hot water from the stove, quickly washed up and put the clean dishes away. She rubbed down the table and made some more coffee. A quick glance at Shannon showed she was asleep, so Bella tiptoed out of the house and headed in the direction of the barn.

Brian looked up as she approached, his smile making her heart race.

"Bella, there you are. Did Shannon make you run away with her chatter?" Brian teased.

"No. She fell asleep. I was worried I would wake her, so I came out here." Bella glanced around them. "Are you finished?"

"Almost. Are you ready to go back to town?"

Bella wasn't. She was enjoying her time with Brian and his friends. But Shannon was unlikely to rest properly with guests, so it was only fair to leave.

"I think Shannon could do with some rest," she said.

"We can come back another day," Brian said, as if reading her mind. "I think the two of you will become quite good friends. I can tell that she likes you a lot."

Bella blushed. She found it difficult to believe people liked her just for herself.

"I hope you stay in Riverside Springs," he added, before turning away to check the horse.

Bella wondered if he was saying that for Shannon's sake or because he liked her?

CHAPTER 41

BELLA

The next two weeks passed quickly. Shannon promised to order a dress after the baby came and, in the meantime, she helped to drum up new business by telling all the farmers' wives about Bella. Mrs. Grayson suggested she make a couple of dresses to hang in the window. That way she may tempt people when they came into the store to buy other items.

Bella soon had more than enough work to keep her busy. Every day flew by, and in the evenings, she either sat with Mrs. Grayson and chatted or she went walking with Brian. He explained that he couldn't get to town every day due to his commitments on his farm, but he always made time for her when he could.

Mrs. Grayson couldn't do enough for Bella and for that she was very grateful. She wrote to Lily to tell her of her good fortune and also enclosed a letter for Kathleen telling her how well their new business venture was turning out. She had run through some plans for when Kathleen came to join her. There wasn't enough income yet to support the two of them, which worried her a little. When Mrs. Grayson saw her frowning, she told her off. "Bella, you got to trust things will work out for the best. They usually do."

Bella wasn't about to argue. But in her experience, good things didn't last. So, despite her happiness, she couldn't get rid of the feeling that all was not well.

"BELLA ARE YOU IN THERE?"

"Yes, Mrs. Grayson. Just a minute," Bella answered as she finished the seam she was sewing. She hated stopping in the middle.

"I know you hate being interrupted, but you got a letter. I thought you might want to read it. It's from Mud Butte."

Mrs. Grayson held out the letter, her concern for Bella obvious. Bella's nightmares had returned with a vengeance and she had woken the older woman with her screams more than once. Mrs. Grayson had told her a problem shared was a problem halved but she hadn't been able to put her fear into words.

Hands shaking, Bella ripped open the letter. She quickly scanned the contents before sitting down. Brian came in just at that moment. "Morning, ladies. I had to come to town for some seed," his voice faltered, "Bella, what's wrong? You look like you saw a ghost."

She looked up at Brian, her hands trembling as she held the letter closer. Her heart was beating so fast, she tried to take a breath, but it wouldn't come.

"Bella, sit down. Take a sip of this," Brian said, handing her a glass of water. "Now, tell me."

"I think the girls are in trouble," she said, knowing she was talking too fast but trying to get the words out of her head. "The orphans, Megan and Eileen, from the train. I just knew there was something horrible with that town. The sheriff and those Maitlands."

"Bella, slow down, you aren't making any sense," Brian said.

Bella explained about the twins and how she felt about their placement. She told Brian about the way the sheriff had behaved too.

"This lady, she was the one who wanted to adopt them. She says she's concerned, but she doesn't want to stir up trouble as her husband and the sheriff have had words before. She says she wrote to me as she saw how close I was to the twins. I told her I would be staying in Riverside Springs. I gave her the address of the mercantile. I just had a feeling I should even though I knew it would be Carl or the Outplacement Society people should contact. I don't know what to do. I wish Bridget hadn't gone back to New York already."

"Oh my," Mrs. Grayson said, taking a seat.

"Can I see the letter?" Brian asked.

She handed it over and watched as his expression grew grim while he read the note.

"It's short but to the point," he said when he'd finished. "I think we should go speak to Reverend Franklin. He may know people in this Mud Butte place."

"That's a good idea. I will look after everything here. Go with Brian, Bella." Mrs. Grayson gave her a quick hug.

Bella took her shawl from the hook by the door and walked out with Brian, her stomach roiling with fear.

CHAPTER 42

BELLA

"*B*rian, I'm scared."

"Don't be, Bella. You have us now." His eyes glowed as he looked at her. "You should know I wouldn't let anything happen to you."

"Thank you," she mumbled.

"We can figure something out. Maybe some of our neighbors know this town. Come on, let's find Reverend Franklin."

Bella looked away. They were outside the store now, but the street was quiet.

"Bella, what is it? There is something you are not telling me isn't there?"

"I can't," she said.

"Yes, you can."

"No, I can't. You might think different about me. The people in Riverside Springs won't want my kind living here."

"What are you talking about? Your kind? You are a lovely young woman and the whole town thinks that. How could you possibly think any different?" he said.

"I was an orphan, on the trains."

"We know, Bridget told us."

"Yes, but what she didn't tell you was that I was abused. By the family that took me in. They beat me and punished me all the time. But when…" Bella's voice faltered as she covered her face with her hands.

"What, Bella?"

"When I turned twelve, the master of the house, he started paying me more attention. I didn't like it. I told him it hurt. He, he…" she couldn't say it. It was too horrible.

Brian paled then turned red, his fists clenched as anger radiated out of him. For a split-second Bella thought he was angry with her, but his words reassured her.

"You are not responsible for anything that happened to you. You were a child. Do you hear me?"

"You're shouting," she said.

Looking ashamed he lowered his voice.

"Sorry, I didn't mean to shout. But it makes me real mad. Bella, you were an innocent child. Nothing that happened to us orphans was our fault. Nobody is going to hold you responsible."

"You really believe that?"

He put his finger under her chin and gently tugged it upward until she was staring into his face.

"Bella Jones, I believe in you. You are kind, talented, and hardworking. Just the type of woman a man would be honored to have as his wife. I think you feel something for me, but you are young, and I have been trying to be patient. I want to have a future with you. So, dry your eyes and let's go see if we can find out what we can do."

"You want me?" she couldn't stop herself from questioning him. She wanted to believe him.

"Yes, I want you. I want to hold you, protect you, and love you for the rest of my life. I want to wake up every morning and see your smiling face. You mean the world to me, Miss Bella Jones."

"Oh!"

He laughed.

"That wasn't the reaction I was hoping for, but it will do for now. Let's go see the Reverend. He's a wise man. But first, you might want to wash your face."

Bella ran into the store and up to her room to do just that. It gave her an excuse to consider what he had said. She hugged herself, he'd told her he cared for her and wanted a future with her. She couldn't stop smiling even though she was worried about the children. Having Brian by her side would help in the days ahead.

CHAPTER 43

KATHLEEN

Kathleen stared out the window as the train pulled into the station. Freesburg was the largest town they had visited since leaving Cheyenne. Miss Screed took the children to meet their prospective parents. Kathleen was about to accompany her before making her way to find the priest. To her surprise, the priest was waiting for her at the station. She quickly made her apologies to Miss Screed and moved to greet the Priest.

"Pastor John sent me a telegram, Miss Collins. I have found your brothers. But I'm afraid the news isn't good. They are in a lot of trouble."

"Trouble?" Kathleen repeated, looking into the priest's troubled eyes. He seemed to be genuinely concerned.

"They have been arrested for murder," he replied.

The sky and ground started to spin, she reached out to stop herself from falling. Richard moved closer to put his arm around her shoulders.

"Perhaps we could go somewhere more private?" Richard suggested. "Miss Screed has Patrick, so I am free to accompany you."

She heard Richard talking but his voice seemed to be coming from far away. Shane and Michael couldn't murder anyone. But then, she didn't think Maura would steal and run away from Lily either. Did she know her family at all?

"Forgive me for being clumsy. I am so sorry," the priest apologized. "Why don't you come to my home beside the church. I can't promise you anything but a cup of coffee."

"Coffee would be lovely, thank you," Richard replied. "I am Doctor Richard Green, I met Miss Collins on the train and am now responsible for one of her previous charges, Patrick."

Kathleen listened to the exchange of greetings and followed Richard to the priest's home without speaking. Only once they were sitting down did she put her thoughts into words,

"But who? How? Shane and Michael wouldn't kill anyone," she said.

"With the greatest respect, are you sure?" Richard asked her. "You said yourself they lived on the streets of New York and were in trouble with the police before they came out here."

The priest didn't comment but seemed intent on studying the table in front of him. Kathleen tried to hold back her anger. It wasn't Richard's fault she was in this mess.

"Doctor Green, my brothers roamed the

neighborhood and fell in with a bad crowd, but they were never guilty of more than stealing some food here or there. I know stealing is wrong, we all knew that. But they were starving. They were picked up by the police on the orders of a man who had a personal vendetta against my sister," she replied coldly. "Father, can you take me to them, please?"

"I am not sure that is wise," he said with a look at Richard. Kathleen wished he would address her. The boys were her brothers, Richard hadn't even met them.

"I need to see my brothers. Will you help me, or do I have to go alone?" Kathleen surprised herself almost as much as the men. She had never been forceful in her life. Living with older sisters like Bridget and Maura, her role had always been that of peacemaker in the family. But these boys were her flesh and blood. When she'd composed herself a little better, she went on in a gentler voice, "I apologize for being rude. I want to see my brothers. I know they didn't do this."

The priest looked to Richard who nodded.

"I will take you, Miss Collins, but you must be prepared," he said. "They likely have changed a bit since you last saw them."

"Would you like me to come with you?" Richard offered.

"Do you believe them to be guilty?" she asked, piercing him with her gaze. When he didn't return her look, she shook her head.

"I will go alone. Thank you."

"First, I suggest you book into a boarding house. I can show you to a clean, respectable establishment. Tomorrow morning, I will collect you and take you to the boys."

Kathleen wanted to go now but she sensed she needed to make herself more amenable if she wished to rely on the Priest's support. She nodded and let him show her the way to her temporary home. Richard came with them, talking to the priest about the town and other matters. Kathleen couldn't concentrate on anything but her brothers.

It didn't take long to reach the Baker

lodging house. Mrs. Baker didn't smile as she greeted them. Kathleen didn't believe it was personal if the frown lines on the older woman's face were anything to go by. She looked as if life had been hard to her.

"Thank you, Father, for your help. I shall be ready early tomorrow." She didn't say a word to Richard but walked slowly up the stairs to her allocated room. She couldn't believe the news. How could Michael and Shane have ended up like this?

After a restless night, she got up early.

Kathleen dressed carefully. Her family's honor was on trial. She needed to prove to the sheriff and judge that her brothers had been brought up properly. Mrs. Baker greeted her when she went downstairs by telling her a parishioner had died and the priest was needed elsewhere.

Kathleen hesitated unsure of what she should do. She glanced at Mrs. Baker, wondering if she should ask the landlady where the jailhouse was but what if she threw her out of her boarding house.

She closed her eyes and thought of Lily and Bridget. They wouldn't stand here wondering what to do. They would take action. Thanking Mrs. Baker and declining breakfast, she pushed the door open and walked into the street, her shoulders back and her head held high. She stopped a couple of ladies on the street and inquired where she could find the sheriff. That sounded better than asking for the jailhouse. They would assume she needed the lawman's services. With a deep breath, she followed their directions. It took twenty-five minutes to reach the jailhouse. Once there, her nerve almost failed her. Could she handle this alone? She didn't have much choice. Her brothers were depending on her and she wasn't about to let them down.

CHAPTER 44

BELLA

*R*everend Franklin hadn't heard anything bad about Mud Butte, but the name of the sheriff did sound familiar to him. The grave expression on his face didn't help Bella's feelings of guilt.

"I think we should go to Mud Butte and find out what is going on," Brian said.

"We can't just go riding in there, Brian. We haven't got any right," Reverend Franklin cautioned.

"No," Brian agreed, then looked at her. "But Bella does."

Confused, Bella looked at him. What right did she have to go asking questions in Mud Butte.

"Sorry, Brian, I'm not following you." The Reverend looked as confused as he sounded.

Relieved the Reverend wasn't following Brian's train of thought either, Bella waited for Brian to explain.

"As far as these people know, Bella worked for the Outplacement Society. She can tell them she's back for an inspection visit."

Bella couldn't believe Brian thought she would be taken seriously as an agent.

"They won't believe that." Reverend Franklin quickly dismissed the suggestion, causing Bella to feel insulted, even though she thought the same.

"And besides, Carl told them he would be back in six months." Reverend Franklin didn't seem to notice he had upset Bella.

"Yes, but plans change. I can wear a suit and tell them I am the new outplacement agent and Bella is showing me the ropes," Brian said. "It could work."

Reverend Franklin looked thoughtful as he scratched his beard.

"I could be leading you into danger," Bella protested. She looked to the Reverend hoping he would talk Brian out of the scheme, but he was nodding his head.

"It could work. After all, if there is nothing wrong and they don't have anything to hide, then why should they mind? If this Mrs. Mac-Donagh is correct, we need to be getting those children away from the family. They are the important ones."

Bella agreed with the reverend, but Brian was important too. She couldn't bear if anything happened to him, not now she knew how he felt about her.

"I'll get Mitch and some of the other men to come with us," Brian added.

"Mitch may not want to come. Shannon is near her time," Bella reminded Brian.

"She has weeks yet. We'll be back in time,"

Brian said confidently. "Geoff Rees is well known around these parts. He is bound to have some contacts with lawmen."

"Oh, good thinking, Brian. He knows the sheriff in Green River. I think they may have grown up together. Geoff can send him a wire." The reverend fell silent for a few seconds before adding, "I'm coming too."

"You, Reverend?" Brian didn't bother to hide his surprise.

"Yes me. I may be old, but I'm not dead." The Reverend clapped Brian on the back. "Now, you ride out for Mitch and I will head to see Geoff. Bella, you better tell Mrs. Grayson. She might pack us some lunch to take with us for the trip. We can't afford to wait for the stage coach. We will ride to Green River and take the train from there."

"I can't ride," Bella squeaked. "I've never been on a horse."

"I'll teach you," Brian said. "Taking a wagon will take too long."

Bella didn't relish the idea of riding, but the reverend saved her.

"No, Brian," he said. "If we're successful, we'll need the wagon to bring the children back with us. We can leave the wagon at the livery in Green River. It will be safe there."

The men went off to gather their respective parties and Bella walked back to the store.

"There you are, dear," Mrs. Grayson said. "I've been going out of my mind worrying about you. What did the reverend say?"

To Bella's consternation, tears ran down her face.

"Bella, sit down. It might not be as bad as you fear."

Bella shook her head, unable to speak. She tried, but the tears kept coming. She hadn't cried for years. Why now?

"Take a few deep breaths, dear."

She did as she was told. Deep breathing helped.

"I shouldn't have left them there," she said.

"You had no choice, Bella. What could you

do when the Outplacement Society made their decision? Carl has years more experience than you. What happens now?"

Quickly, Bella outlined their plan. Mrs. Grayson nodded in agreement.

"I think it's a good one. Who in Mud Butte would suspect you as you are so innocent looking? And Brian could charm the pollen from the bees."

Bella cringed at the word innocent but now was not the time. She could tell Mrs. Grayson her story later. She had to get ready to go. She repeated the reverend's request for some food then went upstairs to pack a small bag. She didn't know how long they would be gone. Once she came back down, Mrs. Grayson hugged her close. "Bella Jones, you look after yourself. You are a very special young woman. Never forget it."

Bella couldn't believe what she was hearing. Nobody had ever called her special before.

CHAPTER 45

BELLA

The trip to Mud Butte took nearly a week. Bella fretted the whole time, worrying they would be too late to rescue the girls.

"It will be fine, Bella. Have faith." Reverend Franklin kept telling her.

Faith in what? She didn't want to ask. She considered writing to Bridget and Father Nelson but, in reality, by the time they got the letters, the situation would be resolved one way or another. Geoff Rees had come with them.

His legal knowledge would prove handy. She just hoped they wouldn't need his gun.

They reached Mud Butte late on Friday evening. It was exactly a month since Bella had left. She hoped she wouldn't bump into the sheriff. Geoff Rees took them to a different hotel, which was slightly more upmarket than the one they had stayed in when they first came to the town. Brian offered to accompany Bella to the Macdonough's place. He had asked around town where he might find it. She wondered if they were being silly to be so cautious, but her instincts told her they should avoid the sheriff.

They rented a wagon and drove out to the MacDonagh place. It was smaller than Brian's land but looked well maintained. The house had a small garden out front with some flowering plants covering the wall of one side of the house. The door opened at the sound of their approach. She was surprised to see Mr. MacDonagh with his gun.

"Mr. MacDonagh, my name is Bella Jones. We met a while back."

He didn't get a chance to answer as his wife came out.

"Oh, Miss Jones, thank you for coming. Sorry about greeting you with a gun, but we've reason to be fearful." Gracie came forward wringing her hands. "I didn't know if I was doing the right thing writing to you, but I just couldn't bear it if anything happened to those girls."

"This is my friend, Mr. Brian Curran," Bella said. "We brought more friends, they're in town right now."

Mr. and Mrs. MacDonagh exchanged a quick look.

"Why don't you come inside for some coffee and my wife can tell you what she knows," Mr. MacDonagh said.

"What we know, Giles," his wife corrected him quietly.

Bella and Brian walked inside. The interior looked very similar to the house the Maitland's had but with one big difference. It was obvious this was a home. Gracie had made a rag rug for the floor as well as chairback covers for each chair. There were pretty curtains on the windows and Bella saw a beautiful quilt on the bed as the bedroom door was ajar. It looked cozy, though devoid of any luxury items.

"We debated whether we should write to you. I'm not afraid for myself, but for my wife," Mr. MacDonagh said. "Gracie has such a kind soul, and the sheriff and his friends, the Maitlands, aren't the type of people I want her to be mixing with."

"The sheriff?" Brian asked.

"I don't have any proof, but I believe the sheriff knows the Maitlands mistreat those children. None of them are theirs to start with. They are all orphans. They don't live in the house either, they stay in the barn."

"The barn?" Bella whispered.

"Yes, ma'am. We didn't know the girls had been adopted by them. They usually stick to boys, apart from one girl I saw when I dropped off some goods for the store." He took a loud deep breath. "I took Gracie home as she was so upset at not being able to adopt both those girls. I wish I had let her now. I should have let her."

"Giles, it's not your fault," Mrs. Mac-Donagh said. "You were right. We can't afford two children."

Bella couldn't believe her ears. Everything they had been told was a lie. No wonder Susan had looked so uncomfortable when they visited. The poor child.

CHAPTER 46

KATHLEEN

*K*athleen pushed open the jailhouse door. A grumpy looking man in need of a bath sat behind the main desk. There was another desk against the far wall. A wood stove and a coffee pot were the only other furnishings. The floor was filthy and, judging by the number of dead flies on the window sills, a cleaner rarely visited.

Except for the fact the man present was wearing a badge, she would have assumed he was a prisoner. The wall behind him was covered in wanted posters.

"What can I do for you, pretty lady?"

He didn't stand. She didn't like the look in his eyes. She drew a deep breath knowing she had to keep her wits about her. In her mind, she pictured how Lily would deal with this man.

"I believe you have my brothers, Michael and Shane Collins, in custody. I would like to see them."

She was glad her voice was firm and thankful her skirts hid her shaking legs. The man's gaze roved over her from her head to her toes.

"I don't think they're up to visitors." He sneered, speaking to her chest.

Her cheeks flushed with temper. Kathleen bit back her anger. She wouldn't get anywhere with this man by trying to be forceful. She had to remain calm and in control of her voice.

"Please, sir, I haven't seen them in over a year. Just for a few minutes. Then I can go back and tell my family I saw them. It would make me so happy." She forced herself to look in his eyes and smile.

His gaze raked her from head to foot, but she refused to let him see he intimidated her. She forced herself to breathe shallowly, his body odor making her eyes water. She stared at a point just above his shoulder. He exhaled sharply before taking a key from his person.

"You got ten minutes, lady."

The sheriff spat his tobacco, his aim falling well short of the spittoon. He stood and opened the door to the back where the cells were. He indicated she follow him. The hallway was extremely dark, and he walked too close to her. Belatedly, she wished she had asked for Richard to accompany her but how should she have known she might need protecting from a lawman. He stopped at one of the cells. Taking out a large ring of keys from his pocket, he opened it and stood back, motioning her to move inside. Cringing at the stench, she pushed open the metal door into the cell.

"Oh my," she cried out in surprise when she saw them. "What happened to you?"

Both her brothers were black and blue.

Their eyes were swollen closed. Michael had a nasty looking cut above his left eye and held his arm awkwardly. Shane wasn't in a much better state. She moved from one to the other, the state of them not stopping her from hugging them both. They had never been overweight but now she could feel the bones protruding. They hadn't been fed properly.

"What are you doing here, Kathleen?" Michael asked, his tone not too welcoming.

"I came to find you," she said. "You didn't write, and I got worried."

"Wasn't much time for writing. Not where we were."

She ignored Michael's sullen tone and instead addressed Shane.

"How did you end up here?"

He looked at her sadly for a couple of seconds before Michael answered for him.

"You don't want to know."

"Michael John Mary Collins, you listen to me. I haven't crossed state lines to listen to you treat me like a kid. I'm here to help. Why does the sheriff think you murdered someone?"

"Don't think nothing, lady. I got witnesses," the sheriff said behind her, making Kathleen jump a little. She hadn't realized he was still standing there.

"You don't got nothing," Michael retorted.

Kathleen's cheeks heated as her brother let out a string of curse words at the sheriff who retaliated in kind.

"Gentlemen, please."

All heads turned to the door. Kathleen was relieved Richard had ignored her instructions to leave her be.

"How you talk to each other is your own business. But don't subject a lady to listening to that filth. Why haven't these men seen a doctor?"

The sheriff shrugged his shoulders. "Didn't see the need. Not when they'll be dangling at the end of a rope soon enough.

Kathleen gripped the bar of the cells. How

could the sheriff talk about their deaths so casually?

"The judge hasn't heard the case yet. They're innocent until proven guilty. They need medical attention, a bath, and new clothes."

The sheriff spat another stream of tobacco juice onto the floor. Richard gave him a filthy look, but the lawman ignored him.

"Soft-hearted city boys. That's all I need. Get out! I got a town to keep safe. I don't have time to be acting as nursemaid to two murderers," the sheriff said.

"We told you before, we didn't kill nobody. It was Beaugrand, and if you weren't on his payroll you would see that," Michael retorted.

The sheriff took a step into the cell toward Michael, a menacing look in his eyes, his hand resting on his gun, "What did you say to me, boy?"

Kathleen put herself between the sheriff and her brothers.

"My brothers need a lawyer," she said. "Have they seen one?"

"Nobody stupid enough to touch their case around here. They ain't got a cent between them, and lawyers like to be paid." The sheriff spat on the floor. "Your time is up, get out."

"But they need medical—"

"Get out," he repeated. "This is my jail and my town. I give the orders around here."

Kathleen was going to argue but Richard pulled her away.

"Come on. We can't do anything here," Richard told her.

"I can't—" Kathleen protested.

"Kathleen, come with me. We need to talk. In private," he told her, dropping his voice.

"Michael, Shane, I will be back. I promise," she said as Richard pulled her out of the cell.

"Kathleen, go home. Forget you ever saw us. There's nothing you can do for us," Shane said sadly before turning his head to look away from her.

With those words ringing in her ears, she picked up her skirts and fled the jail.

CHAPTER 47

KATHLEEN

*O*nce they were outside, Richard caught up with her. She wasn't able to run fast in her skirts. And as it was, she was attracting attention.

"Kathleen, wait. We have to discuss this."

"You heard what the sheriff said," she told him. "He won't even let you see to them. I swear Michael's arm is broken."

"Yes, given the angle he was holding it at, I agree," Richard agreed. "But you and I arguing isn't going to help anyone. We have to engage an attorney."

"I don't have the money for one of those," Kathleen said.

"I do. Come on, let's go find one."

"I can't let you pay for everything," she said, feeling nervous. "You've already been generous enough. Especially looking after Patrick."

"I can afford it," he assured her. "My grandfather left me very well off. Now, please, stop wasting time and let's find an attorney."

Kathleen took his proffered arm and together they walked down the street looking for a lawyer. The first two they visited more or less laughed them out of their offices.

"This is no use. Nobody will help us," Kathleen said before she had a thought. "Wait, I need to send a telegram."

"To whom?"

"Charlie Doherty," she said. "He works for an attorney in New York. He may be able to recommend someone."

"Worth a chance, I guess," Richard said.

"The telegraph office is right around that corner."

Together, they sent a telegram giving Kathleen's boarding house as the reply address.

"What do we do now?" Kathleen asked.

"I think you should go and lie down. You've had a shock and look tired. I will call on a couple of doctors and see if I can find out who is who in this town. I want to know who this Beaugrand guy is. I don't like hearing the sheriff is friendly with the guy your brothers accused of being the real villain."

"So, you believe them? My brothers, I mean?" Kathleen said hopefully.

"I don't know your brothers." He took her hands gently. "But I am getting to know you, and I believe you believe they aren't capable. So, for now, that is enough for me to try to help."

"Thank you, Richard." She was too choked up to say anything else.

"Now, off you go and rest. The next few days will be difficult."

She didn't reply. She couldn't begin to imagine how the next few days and weeks would play out.

CHAPTER 48

BELLA

*B*ella and Brian sat at the MacDonaghs' table listening as the couple told them everything they knew.

"But Jack told us his child died and everything," Bella said, trying to work out what was truth and what was deception on the part of the Maitlands.

"They did have a child die on them, but it wasn't at the same time as the Lord took our Matilda Rose," Giles faltered. "A whole lot of people died in that epidemic. But the child who died at the Maitlands died long before that."

"How can the townspeople allow them to carry on taking children?" Bella demanded, causing Giles MacDonagh to look guilty.

"They're powerful folk when they get together," he said. "There's them two brothers, and the sheriff, and the store owner. There may be more. But that's a lot of people in a relatively small town like this. We got our own problems, Miss Jones. Not saying that excuses us, but..."

Bella noticed his neck going red. She could see he was ashamed and, while part of her remained angry, she was also reasonable enough to realize they were in a difficult position.

"I tried speaking to the sheriff once. He told me to mind my own business or he may have to take Gracie away." Mr. MacDonagh took his wife's hand and held it tight. "My Gracie was so ill after we lost Tilly Rose then we lost another baby. I thought she would die of a broken heart. Sheriff said he thought she lost her mind. He said he would have her put in an institution. I couldn't risk that."

Everyone fell silent, the only sound in the room was labored breathing as they each tried to keep their emotions in check. Bella wanted to scream, rant and rave, but most of all she wanted to cry. What had Megan and Eileen lived through since she had seen them last?

"I am so sorry for all you have been through, yet you had the confidence to write to Bella." Brian said.

"We decided we're going to leave Mud Butte. It has nothing for us but bad memories. We were going to sell up and move into Green River. I should be able to find work. Gracie felt it was the right time to write to you. She said from the start you wouldn't stand for anything bad happening to those girls." He glanced at Bella then continued, "She didn't tell me until after the letter was gone. My wife is a brave woman and she is right. We heard some bad stories. A man I know was offered a young girl at the saloon. The description of the man doing the offering sounded a lot like Jack Maitland."

Bella bit her lip in an effort not to cry out.

"Those kids need help. We were wrong not to take a stand before." Giles looked at Bella. "I can't tell you how sorry I am."

"You don't have any need to apologize, Mr. MacDonagh. You were protecting your family. That's how it should be," Brian said firmly. "But now there are enough of us to take on the Maitlands and their friends."

"Brave words, but it will take more than just the four of us," Mr. MacDonagh said, "Please call us Gracie and Giles."

"Remember those friends we mentioned?" Brian said. "One has already wired the sheriff in Green River."

"I sure hope he didn't use the telegraph office in town," Giles said, looking nervous. "The operator and the sheriff are really close."

CHAPTER 49

BELLA

*B*rian drove the wagon with Bella and Gracie riding in the back. Giles rode his horse in case he needed to come back to his farm. They drove up to the hotel. Bella and Brian walked into the hotel to find their friends waiting for them. They quickly introduced Gracie and Giles to Geoff, Mitch, and the Reverend.

"Did you get a wire back from Green River?" Bella asked Geoff Rees.

"Yes," Geoff replied. "Help is on the way, but we need to wait for backup before we act."

"We can't do that. The MacDonaghs have told us the girls are being kept locked in a barn and treated like livestock. But that might not be the worst of it. There are some ugly rumors flying around. We need to go out there and take them home." Bella knew she was speaking loudly but she couldn't help it. She had to convince them to go today. They had waited long enough.

"We can't do that, Miss Jones, we don't have any authority. If we go riding onto the Maitlands' land, they're within their rights to shoot us. We need to wait for the Green River sheriff to get here. He will have the authority we need," Geoff Rees said firmly.

Gracie took Bella's hand and led her to the side of the room.

"We can't do anything to risk those children. We have to have patience," Gracie said soothingly.

"I can't bear to think of what they are going through." Bella sat then stood again.

"Don't let your imagination run away with you," Gracie warned.

Bella didn't have to use any imagination. She had lived through enough of her own horrors to know exactly what the girls might be subjected to. But she couldn't admit that to Gracie, not just because she was a stranger, but she was sure the woman felt bad enough already.

"Mr. Rees, how did you manage to send a wire without warning the sheriff? He and the telegram operator are close," Mr. MacDonagh said.

Mr. Rees grinned as he took out a ten-dollar bill. "A few of these helped."

Bella gasped. "You bribed him? I think that's against the law."

"It is, Miss Jones, but after I explain why to Stuart William, the Green River Sheriff, I don't think he will hold it against me. I met with Sheriff Slater and he is just as bad as you said he was and a whole lot more. I wouldn't trust him with a hundred-year-old goat, never mind to act in the best interests of a child."

The time passed so slowly. Nobody could eat or sleep. They sat around talking or the men paced while the women chatted. Brian came over to check on Bella a few times, but she was too wound up to talk to anyone. She counted the hours. Just how long did it take a sheriff to get from Green River to this town? They agreed not to walk around in town for fear they would spook the Maitlands. Waiting was bad enough but being stuck inside made it worse. She sat to write a letter to Kathleen care of Lily. Lily had agreed to forward her letters to Kathleen as soon as Kathleen sent her an address. She didn't say too much about the twins as she didn't want to alarm her friend who was too far away to help. Sucking the pencil, she tried to put her fears aside and concentrate on Kathleen and her adventures. Had she found her brothers yet?

CHAPTER 50

KATHLEEN

Surprised to find she did sleep, Kathleen woke up late afternoon feeling better. She washed, dressed, and went downstairs to check whether she had any telegrams. Charlie not only answered but said he had sent a telegram to an acquaintance in town and asked him to help. The acquaintance, Randolph James, had called to see Kathleen. Mrs. Baker gave her his contact details. She wondered if she should wait for Richard but decided she didn't have much time to lose.

After getting directions from Mrs. Baker, she walked to Mr. James's office. Her spirits fell as she surveyed the vision in front of her: peeling paint and a sign that needed new letters, unless Mr. Randolph James had decided to use "Rand Ja" as his business name. She knocked on the door. Hearing a muffled reply, she pushed the door open.

"Oh." She couldn't help the remark. The office was strewn with pieces of papers and books on every conceivable surface, even the chairs. It looked like a tornado had hit the small space.

"Mr. James? My name is Kathleen Collins."

"Do come in," he called to her. "Please excuse the mess. My secretary resigned a few weeks ago and I am in rather a muddle."

Kathleen walked into the office, careful not to step on anything. Mr. James was a lot older than she'd expected. He looked like a grandfather from a book, rather eccentric with his mismatched tie and suit.

"Your friend Charlie works for an old student of mine," he told her. "He said you were in trouble but didn't give me much more to go on. Will you please take a seat?"

She looked around, making him laugh self-consciously. He pulled some papers and books off a chair then, when she was seated, he sat on the edge of his desk.

"So, how can I help, Miss Collins?"

"My brothers need legal representation. They are currently in the jailhouse."

"What have they done?" he asked.

"I don't think they did anything, but the sheriff has charged them with murder."

"Ah." Mr. James's eyebrows met his overhanging hair.

"My brothers are good boys," Kathleen protested, then feeling she should be honest went on with, "Well, they were mostly good boys. They ran a little wild when my parents died. But it was New York, and everyone was starving. I don't believe they would kill anyone."

"How did they end up here in Freesburg?" he asked.

"They came on the orphan train. I thought they were working on a farm, but I haven't heard from them since they left a year or so ago. I came out here to make sure they were doing all right."

"So, you had your suspicions they might be in trouble?"

Kathleen didn't want to admit that. "I wanted to see them again. I missed them."

He looked at her shrewdly, so she wasn't sure he believed her.

"Who did they kill?" At her cough, he amended his question. "That is, who are they supposed to have killed?"

She stared at him for a couple of seconds.

"I don't know. I didn't ask. I went to see them, but I got really upset. They have been beaten up and I think Michael's arm is broken. Richard wanted to examine them, but the horrible sheriff wouldn't let him. He said there was no point as they would soon be at the end of a rope. So, I telegraphed Charlie Doherty. I didn't know what else I should do."

Kathleen stopped speaking. She waited for him to say something, but he seemed deep in thought. After a few seconds, he asked.

"Did the sheriff say anything else?"

"No, but Michael accused him of being on the payroll of someone called Beaugrand."

"Ah," Mr. James said.

Kathleen waited for him to elaborate but, when he didn't, she prompted him. "What does that mean?"

"How many attorneys have you been to visit Miss Collins?"

"A few," she said noncommittally. She didn't want to admit he was their last hope.

"I am guessing nobody wanted to take on the case."

"No, they didn't." She shifted in her seat, becoming uncomfortable. Was he going to turn them down too?

"Did they tell you why?" he asked.

"No, sir. Maybe they thought I didn't have the money to pay them. They would be right but, Richard, he's the doctor who was on the train I came on—it's a long story—he said he would meet the costs," Kathleen said.

"I doubt he has enough money to convince any attorney to go up against Beaugrand. Not in this town."

"Why? He's only a man, isn't he?" Kathleen hoped she sounded more confident than she felt.

"He's a very powerful man who happens to own most of the land in this county. The town is named after his mother, her maiden name was Freesburg. She was a foreigner and, from all accounts, didn't have the best welcome when she arrived in the USA. This is his way to honor her."

"He should concentrate on being a decent human being to honor his mother. Wouldn't that be better than naming a town after her?" Kathleen asked.

"I gather most people would think that but as far as Beaugrand goes, there is nobody else worthy in this world but him."

"Oh." Kathleen tried not to cry. Her brothers' chances looked worse than before.

"Don't be upset, Miss Collins. You came to the right office."

"You mean you'll take the job?" While she was glad he was considering it, she wondered why. Could it be that nobody else would employ him?

"I will. And with relish," he said. "It's about time someone showed Beaugrand we are not all on his payroll."

"Mr. James, can I ask why? If nobody else will risk going up against this man, why would you?"

"It would be my last case, Miss Collins. I am retiring, about twenty years too late. My daughter lives in Boston and has been asking me to come live near her for years now. I would like to spend time with my grandchildren. Nothing to keep me in Freesburg now.

Not anymore." His gaze drifted out the window in the direction of the graveyard.

She didn't say anything but let the silence linger between them. Then he seemed to pull himself together as he wiped his hair back from his eyes.

"If I am going to represent them, I best get their statements. Now, where did I put my notebook?"

Kathleen looked around her and saw a pad lying under some books.

"Is this it?" she asked, holding it out to him.

"Yes, thank you," he said, taking the offered notebook. "Say, what are you doing in Freesburg?"

"What do you mean?" she asked, wondering if he was quite sane. She had just explained why she was in the town.

"I mean, do you have a job? You wouldn't consider working for me, would you? I can't afford to pay you, but I can reduce the bill in return for your help around the office. I can also offer you room and board. I have a house-keeper, Mrs. Wainright, who is almost as old as I am. Don't tell her that, of course. My rattling big old house is too big for just the two of us. It would be respectable. What do you think?"

He smiled at her. She had warmed to him immediately.

"You, Mr. James, have a deal." She held out her hand and smiled.

Mr. James took her to see his house where she met his housekeeper. The old woman did indeed look ancient, but the house was beautiful. It was also very big.

"It was different when my family was young, and my wife was here," Mr. James said.

She looked up at the picture in the room. "She was very beautiful."

"Inside and out," Mr. James confirmed. "She didn't stand for any nonsense. There is no way Beaugrand and his friends would have taken over the town if my Clarissa were still alive. How I miss her."

Kathleen didn't say anything. She could

see he was upset. How wonderful it must be to have a man love you so much.

"Right, let's get you situated. Mrs. Wainright will show you to the guest bedroom. Here is a key for you. I have something to do but will meet you at the jailhouse in an hour."

Kathleen thanked him and followed Mrs. Wainright to her new accommodations. The room was larger than any bedroom she had ever seen with a magnificent four poster bed. It was beautifully furnished, the floors and pieces of furniture glistening. There wasn't a speck of dust to be seen.

"It's beautiful. Thank you."

"I'm glad you are here," Mrs. Wainright said. "The old man has perked up. He is livelier than I have seen him in a long time. I hope you will be comfortable here, Miss Collins. Stephanie, our maid of all work, will be here in the morning if you need anything."

"Thank you, Mrs. Wainright. I have to collect my things from the boarding house and meet Mr. James so I won't be back until later."

"You take your time, and watch yourself," Mrs. Wainright replied. "That Beaugrand is a nasty individual. You mark my words."

CHAPTER 51

BELLA

Giles, Mitch, and Brian got talking about the state of farming. All three had suffered their fair share of hardship, including Brian almost losing his dream of having his own farm because of cattle rustlers. Both he and Mitch had overcome their problems, but they still sympathized with the MacDonaghs. They suggested they consider buying a small place in Riverside Springs rather than moving to Green River.

"Couldn't live in a big town after living out in the country myself. Can't imagine how

Bridget and Carl can bear to go back to New York even if it was my birthplace. With all those people and buildings, it's a wonder they can breathe," Brian said.

"We haven't got much option. Even if the property sells, we owe most to the bank. Not much credit on offer from the banks," Mr. MacDonagh added. "I'm hoping to secure work with accommodation."

With each passing hour, Bella fought harder not to scream. How could they speak about work and farming while the children could be suffering?

Finally, Sheriff Williams from Green River arrived with two of his deputies. After greeting Geoff Rees with a big smile, and being introduced to the rest of the group, he asked them to sit down.

"I ain't got good news for you good folks. It appears those Maitland brothers have quite a reputation. Only they weren't always known as Maitland, they have had various aliases. I'm surprised the sheriff is involved though. Never had any complaints about him before."

"He had some money problems a while back. Had a gambling issue or something," Mr. MacDonagh volunteered. "I don't like speaking ill of people, but I do know he is still gambling."

"It wouldn't be the first time the Kingston brothers bribed a law man, but let's make this the last," Sheriff Williams said.

"What are the Maitlands, I mean Kingstons wanted for, Sheriff?" Gracie asked.

"I'm not sure you want to know, Mrs. Mac-Donagh. Some things are not for ladies' ears."

"I want to know how we're going to rescue the girls. The twins came on the train with me and I promised I wouldn't let anything bad happen to them," Bella spoke up, although she hid her hands in her skirts.

"Bella, you couldn't stop what happened. All we can do now is make sure those men aren't able to do the same again." Brian reassured her with a smile before asking, "What's the plan, Sheriff?"

"I need some more deputies. And before you go volunteering, you should know both men are good shooters."

"Don't matter. Those kids need help and we're all they got," Brian said firmly as he volunteered. Mitch didn't think twice and neither did Geoff Rees, but when Reverend Franklin stepped forward, Sheriff Williams shook his head.

"Sorry, Reverend, but I don't think so."

"I aim to go whether I'm wearing a badge or not," the reverend said. "If anyone does get hurt, including those men, they may want a minister to say their last words."

The expression on the sheriff's face suggested praying was the last thing the Kingston/Maitland brothers would be doing, but he didn't say anything.

"We think there may be more children there than the ones you met," Sheriff Williams said, pushing his hat back. "According to folk in town, there could be up to twenty. There are two properties, so we'll split up and hit both at once. Geoff, you'll lead the second group on Joe's property while I take Jack."

"I'm coming too," Bella said, stepping forward.

"As am I." Gracie MacDonagh moved to Bella's side.

"No, ladies, you have to stay here." Reverend Franklin ordered.

"I am coming, and you can't stop me," Bella said firmly, pushing aside her fear. Megan and Eileen needed her. "I want to help with the children. I was an orphan train child and, believe me, Sheriff, there is nothing you can tell me that will shock me. I'll follow you, so unless you arrest me and chain me here I suggest we get going."

"All right," Sheriff Williams said. "But you stay behind at all times and do as you're told."

Bella and Gracie both nodded.

CHAPTER 52

KATHLEEN

athleen was settling her account with Mrs. Baker when Richard walked into the boarding house.

"Where are you off to?" he asked, glancing at her bag.

"I hired an attorney, found myself a job, and a new place to live. I told Miss Screed I won't be accompanying her on the rest of her journey. I don't think she was too sad to see the back of me."

Richard grinned at her words before offering to accompany her to her new lodgings.

He carried her small case as they walked the short distance.

"How is Patrick," she asked.

"I took him to see the doctor and he agrees with me. Patrick's hands will recover with only slight scarring. The doctor has a boy of Patrick's age, so I left him there to find out what is happening with you. I take it you are staying here in Freesburg for the foreseeable future."

"Yes, I am. I don't know how long it will take to clear my brothers' names."

"And if you don't?" he asked.

She didn't want to consider that eventuality. "I will," she responded, crossing her fingers in the folds of her skirt.

"So, tell me more about this attorney," Richard said.

Kathleen explained about Charlie's telegram, her meeting with Mr. James, and his reasons for taking the case.

"Are you sure he's up to the job?" Richard asked.

"We don't have a choice," she said. "Charlie Doherty recommended him, and I trust Charlie. Anyway, no other attorney in this town would touch the case. They all seem afraid of this Beaugrand guy."

"With reason," Richard said. "I made some inquiries around town. He seems to rule the place with an iron fist."

"He needs to realize he lives in America. We have our laws and freedoms and they apply to everyone. I am not going to let any man intimidate me," Kathleen said.

The clapping sound behind her made her squirm. She turned to face a well-dressed, hard-faced man of about forty years.

"Nice sentiment. I take it you are Miss Collins. I am—"

"I know who you are, Mr. Beaugrand." Kathleen guessed he was the man she'd been discussing with Richard. When he didn't correct her she continued, desperate to prove she wasn't afraid of him. "You're the man trying to

341

murder my brothers. You won't succeed, do you hear me?"

She stood facing him, thankful Richard was with her. Her brothers were depending on her, so she stood her ground.

"I'm not looking to murder anyone. On the other hand, your brothers killed a man in cold blood, and they'll be hanged for their crimes."

"Not until a judge finds them guilty," Kathleen said. "I shall see you in court. Good afternoon."

Kathleen turned on her heel and walked on, catching a glance of admiration from Richard. They reached Mr. James' house. Richard waited while she put her bag in her new room then he accompanied her to the jail. They found Mr. James there in a heated argument with the sheriff. She was glad she had met Mr. James before now. He was very angry and quite formidable as he gave the sheriff a piece of his mind.

"Good, you've arrived," Mr. James said when he saw Kathleen and Richard approach.

"I take it this is the doctor? I want you to carefully examine both lads and make a detailed report of their injuries. We will provide the judge with a copy. At least this way, we save your brothers from falling over or otherwise hurting themselves. Isn't that right, Sheriff?"

The sheriff didn't reply but spat on the floor, barely missing the attorney's feet. Kathleen hid a grin as the older man barely concealed his disgust at the sheriff.

The boys were in better form.

"I can't believe you came back. I thought you would get the train straight out of here," Shane said, smiling at her.

"We're family, and families stick together," Kathleen told him. "Richard is going to examine you. I got you new clothes and this here is Mr. James. He's your attorney. He needs to know everything that happened."

"Why? It's a done deal. You know we don't stand a chance in this town," Michael said sullenly. He hadn't even bothered to stand.

"That's right, young man," Mr. James piped in.

"What? You can't just accept their fate. You have to fight it," Kathleen protested.

"I know that, young lady," Mr. James retorted.

Kathleen blushed. She had been rude and disrespectful jumping to conclusions.

"I have been a member of the bar for more years than I care to remember," Mr. James explained. "I have requested a change of venue. To somewhere more impartial."

"Oh." Kathleen knew she should apologize but he was already talking.

"Right, now, boys, you need to tell me the truth. And I mean every word of the story. I don't want any surprises in that court room. Understand?"

"Yeah," the boys mumbled. They all jumped when Mr. James roared at them.

"That's 'yes, sir,'" he thundered. "I'm serious. Any hint of you lying to me and I will resign as your attorney and you can take your chances. Do we understand each other?"

"Yes, sir," the boys said in unison.

Kathleen exchanged a quick look with Richard. Maybe her choice of attorney was the right one after all.

"Once the doc is finished, I will listen to your story. In private, Sheriff."

The sheriff looked as if he had chewed on a lemon, but he didn't argue.

For the first time since she had found out about her brothers, Kathleen felt hope.

CHAPTER 53

BELLA

They followed the group until they were close to the boundaries of the first farm. Brian followed Geoff Rees to the second property with Giles showing them the way. Mitch stayed with the Green River sheriff.

"Ladies, you wait here," Sheriff Williams said. "Don't come anywhere near the house until we call for you. Understood?"

The women stayed silent.

"It's important. I don't want anyone shooting you by accident," Sheriff Williams insisted.

"Yes, sir, we will wait here," Gracie answered, presumably thinking she was speaking for both of them. Bella made no such promise. If Megan needed her, she was going to go in there regardless of who told her not to.

The time passed slowly. Bella fidgeted, wishing she could walk around but that may attract attention. Gracie sat watching the horizon. The first gunshot made them jump. It was quickly followed by several more.

Gracie started praying but Bella didn't join in. She moved closer to the house.

"Where are you going?" Gracie protested.

"I can't just wait here. There has to be something we can do."

Bella started walking toward the sound of the gunshots until the farm came into view. She saw the men were focused on the house, so she made her way to the barn, wondering if the children were there. She opened the barn door carefully.

It appeared to be deserted. She was about

to go out again when she heard a sob then someone shushing.

"Megan? Eileen? Are you here?" Bella whispered.

"Bella, is it you?" Megan crawled out of her hiding place. Bella nearly cried at the sight of the child. She was filthy, and the beautiful grey dress Bella had made for her, was in rags. There were fresh wounds on her legs.

"Oh, Megan darling, come here." Bella moved quickly to scoop the child into her arms. "Where is Eileen? Is she here?"

Megan shook her head.

"Who was with you?"

Megan pointed to what looked like a hole in the wall. Bella released Megan and made her way carefully toward the hole. Poking her head through it, she nearly vomited. The stench was horrific, but the sight was even worse. There were three children of similar age to Megan. Two were ill, they couldn't move from their bed of rags despite their best efforts. The third was standing in the corner, holding a large stick. He looked terrified.

"I am a friend of Megan's and I won't hurt you. I promise," Bella said.

The dark-skinned boy didn't put the weapon down. She wasn't sure he had heard her. "Megan," she whispered. "Can you tell him I am a friend."

"He can't hear you. Let me pass."

Megan entered the hole and Bella followed her. Megan moved closer to the boy and rubbed his arm. The boy looked from Megan to Bella a couple of times. Megan pushed the weapon away and eventually the boy conceded.

"Megan, we have to stay quiet. My friends are here to help you. What other children are here?"

Megan shrugged her shoulders. Bella pulled her toward her again. She cuddled her close, feeling her bones through the fabric. The child must be starving.

Only once the children saw she wasn't a

threat did she move toward the children lying on the bed. They were both sick with high fevers.

"Megan, do you have water?" Bella asked.

Megan shook her head.

"I will have to get some."

Megan clung to her. "Take me."

"I will be back. It's safer for you to stay here."

Megan shook her head furiously.

"Take me," the girl begged.

The gunshots had stopped, but Bella wasn't sure if the battle was over. She didn't want to put the child in danger, but the other children were very ill. She was worried they wouldn't survive much longer.

"Megan, I promise I won't leave you."

"Please don't go."

"Yes, please don't leave. We wouldn't want you to get hurt, would we?" The voice sent shivers down Bella's spine.

CHAPTER 54

KATHLEEN

athleen enjoyed cleaning up the office. She hadn't any experience working with papers before, but it wasn't difficult to put the books back in order on the shelves. She figured out the filing system the previous secretary had used and filed everything she found. Richard called to the office halfway through her second day. He'd told her he was staying in Freesburg until the case was over. Then he would accompany her back to New York. He insisted he had business to take care of back in New York. She didn't know if that was true or not, but she didn't care. It was nice to have a friendly face around this town.

"Looks like you are working hard," he teased as he pointed at her cheek. "You have a black mark right there."

Embarrassed, she rubbed at the spot. "It keeps my mind occupied," she said. "They won't let me see the boys."

"I saw them earlier today. Mr. James, or Randolph as he prefers to be called, insisted. They're better than they were," he said, but the fact he didn't look at her made her nervous.

"Something's wrong."

"Why would you think that?" he hedged.

"I'm not stupid. You can't look me in the face. What did you come to tell me?" she demanded.

"Kathleen, you should sit down."

"I am fine. Tell me."

"Randolph wants to see both of us later to discuss the case in detail, but he agreed to me coming to prepare you."

She took a seat. "This doesn't sound good."

"The good news is the trial venue has been moved to Waterloo and your brothers didn't murder anyone."

"I told you that," she retorted, then immediately apologized. "Sorry, I shouldn't bite your head off. You're only trying to help." She should learn to say less and listen more. She waited for him to speak but he stayed silent.

"Tell me, please."

"Your brothers got involved in a rustling ring," he said.

Kathleen exhaled loudly.

"Cattle rustling is a hanging offense," she whispered as if by saying it quietly it was less horrific.

"Yes, it is." Richard looked at her, a grave expression on his face. "But we may be able to argue the boys didn't know what they were getting involved with."

"May?"

"Kathleen, you should prepare yourself for the worst. Do you want to wire your sisters? Maybe they should come to the trial?"

Kathleen sat in the chair, trying to get a hold of her thoughts. Her brothers would die if found guilty. What should she do? Was there enough time to get Bridget and Carl here? Was that fair when they had other priorities. And what about Maura? She didn't even know where to contact her.

"Kathleen?"

"Sorry. I don't know. I can't think straight. Maybe I should wire them. But I am not even sure where they are. Oh, how could this happen?"

"Kathleen, please don't cry,"

"My brothers will die."

"We haven't lost yet," Richard said. "Why don't you send a wire to your friend in New York? The man who sent you to Randolph. He might know how to contact your sister."

That was a good idea. She should do that, but when she tried to stand her legs felt funny. She sat again.

"Is there no hope?"

Richard looked her straight in the eyes.

"There is always hope, but I think we should be prepared."

"We?" she asked.

"You don't think I would leave you to face this alone."

"But what about Patrick?"

"Patrick is doing fine. His hands are improving, and he is enjoying his time with my friends. He is getting a chance to be a child, although I'm not sure he likes having to attend school every day."

Kathleen imagined he was right. She should really go to see Patrick, but she couldn't concentrate on anything other than her brothers. They must be terrified. She had to be the strong one now.

"And the man who died? Who murdered him?"

"Randolph has a theory on that, but he will tell us more later. In the meantime, what are you going to do?"

"I can't see the boys, so I best get this office finished. Can't have their attorney working in this mess. Where is he anyway?"

"He went to look at the crime scene. Don't worry, he took some men with him. He knows not to venture out alone."

Kathleen stared at Richard. "Is his life in danger?"

"Beaugrand has many friends. It is not in his interest for this trial to go ahead. Don't look so worried, though. Randolph has powerful connections."

Kathleen wished, not for the first time, she had gone to Riverside Springs with Bella. But she couldn't abandon her brothers. They needed her.

CHAPTER 55

BELLA

*B*ella gasped as she looked up to see Alice Maitland staring back at her, Susan by her side. She hadn't heard them come into the barn. Megan shrieked, causing Bella to look from the young girl back to Alice. She pushed the child behind her as she saw the black object in Alice's hand. A gun. Surely the woman didn't plan on using it? She was just carrying it for protection. That had to be it.

"What are you doing here?" Alice snarled, pointing the gun right at Bella's heart. Any doubts she had about the woman's ability to use the gun faded away. Alice's hands weren't shaking.

"I'm taking the children," Bella retorted, anger and fear making her brave. "How could you treat them like this? Those two are really sick and Megan is half starved. What type of woman are you?"

"They aren't ill, they just don't want to work is all. That's right isn't it, Susan?"

Susan nodded, a miserable expression on her face.

"Don't listen, she lies," Megan spat.

"Shut up, you little brat. Been trouble ever since you left her," Alice said.

Bella pulled Megan behind her again to shield her.

"What are you going to do? The sheriff is here to arrest Jack and Joe." Bella refused to show any fear.

"He won't take them. Not if I got you."

Bella gulped. She wished she had listened to the sheriff, but it was too late for regrets. She eyed the gun.

"Don't get any brave ideas. It's loaded, and I know how to shoot."

"If you kill me, you'll hang," Bella said. "There are more men back in town. And a group has gone to get your brother-in-law, if that's what he is. Your best bet is to give yourself up."

"And spend the next ten years in jail." The woman sneered. "I'm getting out of here and you're my ticket."

Megan edged closer to Bella sticking her hands in hers. Bella could feel the child shaking. She wasn't going to desert her again.

She took a step toward Alice. "Why don't you just give yourself up? You must know you can't get away."

"Shut up. Susan, grab the brat. We're taking her with us."

Susan stepped forward to take Megan. Megan screamed, and Bella took advantage of Alice's distraction to lunge for her. Alice recovered quickly but didn't get a chance to fire the gun as Bella hit her and knocked her to the ground. Alice was stronger than she looked but Bella was fighting for something she believed in. The gun lay on the floor out of reach of both of them. Alice grabbed Bella's hair, but it was the blow to the head wound she'd received the night Maura disappeared, that caused Bella to see stars. Her eyes smarted. She couldn't let this woman win. She kicked and squirmed and punched with all her might.

"Megan, run get help," she cried as she tried to get out of Alice's grip. She didn't see Susan pick up the gun until it was too late. The shot rang through the air causing both women to freeze.

"Get up now. Move." Susan swore at Bella before she swung the gun wildly at the sick children. Bella jumped away from Alice, a child with a gun was too unpredictable.

But she didn't realize Susan's intentions until it was too late. The child aimed and pulled the trigger. The blood turned the white blouse crimson. Children screamed as the barn door burst open.

CHAPTER 56

KATHLEEN

*M*r. James arranged to see both Kathleen and Richard in his office that evening at six. Kathleen wore gloves, her fingernails were so badly bitten it was a good job her mam couldn't see her. Mam. What would she make of all this? Maura gone. Annie and Liam adopted, and now her boys fighting for their lives.

"Miss Collins, you have done a magnificent job. I can't remember the last time the office looked or smelt so wonderful," he praised her. "I can even see the carpet for the first time in years."

Pleased at his reaction, Kathleen was glad she had powered through the work. His desk was clear and ready for him to use. His papers were correctly filed and, instead of papers everywhere, you could see the shining wood. Best of all, the room smelled of lavender polish. She took a seat in front of his desk wondering where Richard was.

"Doctor Green was delayed. He will join us shortly. He told me he gave you an update earlier today."

"Yes," Kathleen mumbled, finding it hard to speak.

"I know the news isn't what you wanted to hear but it is better to know what you are facing. I prefer it at least."

"How are Shane and Michael?"

The old man looked at her with pity. "Michael is resigned to what is happening. Between you and me, I suspect he was more aware of what was going on. Shane seems a little bemused."

"Shane always followed our Michael everywhere from the time he could walk, according to Mam." She bit back on the lump in her throat.

"My dear, I know this is very difficult. I will do everything I can, I promise."

She squeezed his hand, unable to speak as she tried to hold back the tears. Richard arrived a few minutes later apologizing for his tardiness. Kathleen got herself under control. She couldn't dissolve into a tearful mess.

"I have a more solid idea of what transpired than before. It appears your brothers were taken in by a rancher named Sachs. He owns a large spread to the north of town. They weren't treated well. The rancher is known for his short temper and maltreatment of both his animals and his staff. The boys complained of being cold and hungry. So, when the opportunity to earn some money came along, they took it."

"Even if it meant breaking the law?" Kathleen interjected but immediately apologized.

"They were approached by a man who claimed to be working for Beaugrand. He owns the largest ranch in these parts. Your brothers claim the man offered them cash in return for looking the other way when some cattle went missing."

Mr. James slurped his coffee before continuing.

"The murdered man, Mr. Diaz, suspected something was up and threatened to report the boys to the authorities. He turned up dead shortly after."

"So, the boys had motive." Kathleen said, not wanting to believe her brothers were guilty.

"Motive, yes, but opportunity is not as evident. Diaz was killed by a single gunshot straight through the heart. Doc confirmed it. His professional opinion is that the shooter was an excellent marksman."

"Neither of my brothers know how to shoot properly," Kathleen said, her voice squeaking.

"Exactly, Miss Collins. So that goes in their favor. Also, they were locked in at night, and therefore it will be difficult for the prosecution to prove they had access to Diaz."

"But if they didn't kill him, who did?" she asked.

"That, my friend, is the big question. There have been some whispers that Diaz tried to blackmail Beaugrand. Diaz was heard boasting that he was going to earn big and head out to California. But all we have at the moment is rumor."

"I guess nobody wants to go into the witness box up against Beaugrand." Kathleen knew she was stating the obvious.

"He is a powerful man in these parts, but there are witnesses to a fight between him and Diaz," Mr. James said.

"Witnesses?" Kathleen questioned, eagerly jumping on what appeared to be good news. "Can't they come forward?"

"The witnesses are your brothers." Richard

said as he entered the room just in time to hear her question.

KATHLEEN COULDN'T BREATHE, her heart was racing, and she felt faint. She stared at the attorney who continued to speak, but she couldn't hear a word he said. His mouth moved but she couldn't focus.

"Drink this, slowly." Richard handed her a glass of water. "Breathe deeply. You have had a shock, and it's only natural to react this way."

"I am sorry to be the bearer of bad news, Miss Collins. I know you love your brothers, and if there was anything I could do to make this easier, I would gladly do it."

"All is not lost yet, Mr. James," Richard said, looking at Kathleen. "I wired some contacts. Having a railroad in the family helps. In the past, Grandfather had to employ some Pinkerton agents. We kept a couple on the payroll. I wired the man in Boise. I don't like Beaugrand."

"Neither do I, he gives me the creeps," Kathleen answered, thinking of the hard-faced man who'd taunted her in the street.

"I believe if he pulled something this shady here, he has done it before. I have the agent working on this theory. Hopefully, we will hear back soon."

"The trial date has been confirmed for next week," Mr. James said. "I hope that man of yours can find something, Doctor. I'd hate to lose the last case of my career."

CHAPTER 57

BELLA

*B*ella held Megan close, the poor child shaking badly with shock as blood pooled around Alice's body. She tried to turn the child's face away from the ugly scene, but Megan seemed transfixed, her eyes glued to Alice. Bella picked her up like a baby and carried her toward the back of the barn where Gracie was helping the other children. Together, they left the horrible scene as a group and, one by one, were lifted onto the wagon.

Sheriff Williams arrested Jack and brought

everyone back to the town. He had sent the undertaker to deal with Alice.

Bella had tried to comfort Susan, but the young girl had been pushed too hard. She had to pull her fingers away from the gun, half afraid Susan would kill herself or someone else. Susan seemed to snap. She began wailing, sounds more suited to a wounded animal than a little girl. She pushed Bella away, wrapping her arms around her body and rocked back and forth.

When the doctor arrived, he had to sedate the poor girl. Bella didn't know what would happen to Susan. The sheriff said he would try to get the judge to see it was self-defense. Bella hadn't commented. If she closed her eyes, she could see Susan take aim and pull the trigger.

The sheriff had taken Susan with him since her presence upset the other children. Megan said it was because she wasn't nice, but that was all she would say. Megan hadn't said a word about her time on the farm, but Bella had seen the marks of abuse when she helped her bathe.

Gracie nursed the other sick children, keeping them cool with wet cloths. They gave Megan and the mixed-race boy, whose name was Charlie, some food.

They sat waiting for Brian and the others to come back. There was still no sign of Eileen. Sheriff Williams had arrested Sheriff Slater and he was in the jailhouse sharing a cell with Jack Kingston, or Maitland, or whatever his name was. Sheriff Williams had left two Green River deputies to guard the prisoners and took the rest as backup to find out what was causing the delay at the other farm.

CHAPTER 58

BELLA

*A*fter what seemed like hours, the men trekked back into town each carrying a child. Bella pushed the hair from her eyes as she searched frantically for Eileen. The little girl had to be safe. She just had to be.

She rushed forward, looking closer at the children. Some were so dirty, it was almost impossible to tell if they were boys or girls. Tears streamed down her face, as terror gripped her. Where was Eileen?

Finally, it was Megan who found her sister. The child ran screaming to a little girl one of

the men had carried past Bella. She hadn't recognized her. Megan clung to her sister's side
despite Bella's efforts to part them. The doctor
came to examine them.

"There is nothing I can do. She's been
starved and has no strength to fight this illness.
I am not even sure what is ailing her." The
doctor scratched his head, pushing his too-long
hair back from his eyes. When he looked at
her, she was shocked to see them swimming in
tears. "If I had seen them earlier, they might
have had a chance but now… it's in God's
hands."

Bella couldn't accept that Eileen would die.
Megan needed her twin, and Bella needed both
girls to survive. Otherwise, the guilt of leaving
them with those horrible men would never
leave her.

She refused to leave their sides except to
use the privy. She sponged Eileen clean, held
her while she was ill, and repeated the process
over and over. At some point, Brian came to
relieve her, but she refused to leave. Gracie

also tried to help but, in fairness, she had her hands full minding the other children. They did everything they could, but the two children who had been ill in the barn died during the first night. A third died the next morning.

Reverend Franklin prayed as did Mitch and Brian. Geoff Rees and the MacDonaghs joined in but Bella couldn't bring herself to say the words. Why had God let this happen? Wasn't He supposed to protect children?

CHAPTER 59

BELLA

The second night passed and, although Eileen gave Bella a fright more times than she cared to consider, she was still breathing the next morning. Megan lay by her twin's side. She couldn't hold Eileen's hand as it seemed to hurt her. But Eileen liked having her sister near. Bella fretted that Megan would fall ill too, but what could she do? Nothing would make Megan leave.

The doctor returned to examine both girls. He didn't hide his surprise at finding Eileen still alive.

"You are doing a wonderful job of taking care of her, Miss Jones," he said as he examined Eileen.

"I'm not doing anything. I just sponge her down, hold her while she is sick, and change the bedding," Bella said.

"Well, something is working as she seems stronger than yesterday," the doctor insisted.

"You mean she won't…"

"She is still very weak," the doctor said softly. She saw the compassion and pity in his eyes. Bella nodded, understanding that he could make no promises about Eileen's future.

"You really should get some rest, Miss Jones. You'll make yourself ill if you don't."

"I'm stronger than I look, Doctor," Bella said, but added in a softer voice, "Thank you."

"If she manages to drink water without vomiting, try giving her some soup. A little at a time. But for now, it is more important she keeps drinking." The doctor turned his attention to Megan who was sleeping. "Has she eaten?"

"Only a little. She won't leave her sister. I've washed her wounds and used some salve Gracie gave me. She made it from herbs from her garden. She said it helps with the healing."

"Gracie MacDonagh is a good woman," the doctor confirmed. "The people who did this to the children deserve to be horsewhipped."

The doctor left without waiting for Bella to react. She wanted to ask him how he felt about the townsfolk of Mud Butte ignoring these children. They might not have known how bad things were at the farms, but they had to know the children weren't being treated properly. They hadn't shown up at school for one thing.

CHAPTER 60

KATHLEEN

The days passed so slowly, Kathleen felt she was counting the seconds not the minutes. Yet all too soon she was on the train to Waterloo. Richard had booked her a room in a respectable boarding house which she could barely afford. He had offered to pay, but she turned him down. He was already laying out large sums for her brothers. She would have to get a job to raise the fare to go home.

When she arrived at the boarding house, there was a telegram waiting for her.

"I told Charlie Doherty where you were staying," Richard confirmed.

Opening the wire, she saw Charlie had transferred some funds to the local bank. A wave of relief hit her. At least that was one less thing to worry about. Richard accompanied her to the bank and soon she had an account opened in her own name.

She was also allowed to visit with her brothers. The courthouse was a massive, two-story building complete with cupola and six massive pillars on its façade. It was pretty intimidating. She walked inside, as the building also housed the jail, to be met by a clean-shaven tall man wearing his badge proudly on his chest. She took it as a good sign, the sheriff in Waterloo was completely different than the one they left behind in Freesburg.

He allowed her to sit in a room with her brothers, although they remained shackled. The three of them were able to catch up on news. Kathleen gave her brothers her letters from

Bridget, enclosing photographs of Annie and Liam taken by their new parents.

"They look happy, don't they?" Shane said.

"Things worked out for them. Not like us," Michael said, his attitude as surly as it had been back in Freesburg.

Kathleen didn't comment. She couldn't afford to fall out with her brothers now and telling them they had only themselves to blame wasn't going to win them over.

"How are you feeling? Are you warm enough? Do you get enough food?"

"What are you? Our mother?" Michael asked. "You should go back to New York. There's no reason for you to stay. Unless you like hangings."

"Michael, stop it. Leave her be. She's only trying to help." Shane turned his attention to Kathleen. "Don't mind him, he's been grumpy since we left New York. Probably was beforehand and I never noticed."

"Colm Fleming was asking for you. He said he missed ya."

"Did he? How's things with him?" Shane asked.

"He got a job on the railroad. Mr. Fleming is working a bit, but most of the time he is looking after Jess and Helen."

"Only a matter of time before they end up on an orphan train too then," Michael sneered.

"Don't be like that. Mrs. Fleming was wonderful to us. Lily will do her best to keep the family together," Kathleen protested.

"Lily didn't do much for us, did she? If she had left us alone, we wouldn't be in this mess."

"That's not true and you know it, Michael. You only have yourself to—" Horrified she had voiced her opinion, Kathleen let her voice trail away. "Sorry."

"You obviously blame me, so why are you here?"

"You're my brothers. What does Mr. James say?"

"He said we have a chance if they find the real killer. If not, we will be dancing in air."

The sheriff chose that moment to tell them

their time was up. Kathleen, although she wouldn't admit it to anyone, was relieved. She and Michael had never been close, but now he was really irritating. She gave Shane a quick hug then left.

CHAPTER 61

BELLA

*B*oth girls were sleeping. Bella pushed the hair from their faces, wishing she could erase the memories of this horrible time. Eileen had sobbed as she told her about how she had been treated. Rebecca, Joe Maitland's wife, had beaten her black and blue and threatened to send her far away. She'd also told her Megan was dead. Poor Eileen had believed the horrible woman and stopped eating, hence she was even thinner than Megan. How could a woman be so horrible to children? According to Eileen, Rebecca had been a hundred times worse than Joe when it came to hurting the children in her care.

A knock on the door startled her.

"Bella, it's only me. I came to bring you some food. I aim to stay here and watch you eat." Brian said quietly but firmly.

She wasn't hungry but when she saw the concern in his eyes, she took the sandwich.

"How are they doing?" he asked as he looked down at the girls.

"Sleeping now. The doctor says Eileen is a little stronger but... he doesn't know what may happen."

"Bella, you've done everything you can," he said quietly.

"But it wasn't enough. I should never have left them," she said.

"You had no choice. How many times do you need to be told that?"

Bella didn't answer. She bit into her sandwich, even though her stomach roiled. She forced herself to eat the food and drink the coffee he had brought her.

"Did you find out how they came to have so many children?" Bella asked. It had been bothering her. Didn't anyone check on the welfare of these kids?

"Seems they were working with a number of agencies, not just the Outplacement one. They had children from the Boston agencies as well as some from a catholic hospital. I reckon the majority of the children they took were ones that would be difficult to place. There aren't many who want a black or Mexican child. Or one who is deaf." Brian looked furious. "The Maitlands hired out the children to other farms. Seems some people didn't care what age they were so long as the work was done."

"But what of the girls? Were they working on the land too?" she asked.

Brian couldn't meet her eyes.

"What? Tell me, please," Bella whispered.

"Seems they were destined for other things. They have had a few girls in the past, some were sent to other places." Brian took a deep breath. "Susan, being older, had already been mistreated. In that way." Brian's neck was bright red as he stared at the floor.

Susan couldn't have been more than ten years old. Bella swallowed hard. She felt dreadful for Susan, but Brian's words had given her a little hope. "You mean… the twins weren't touched?"

"Not as far as we can tell. Rebecca, Joe's wife, has been talking nonstop since they took her in. Seems to think it will help the judge treat her better."

"I hope the judge locks her up forever," Bella retorted. "In fact, she should hang too. She's just as bad, if not worse, than the men."

Brian didn't argue with that.

"She said the twins were treated harshly, particularly Megan as she kept fighting back. When she didn't seem to care what happened to her, they used Eileen to control her. It worked, as Megan couldn't bear to see her twin hurt so she complied."

"She told Eileen, Megan had died. That's why Eileen is so skinny. She stopped eating as she wanted to die too. Oh, thank God we came back when we did." Bella took the rag up and started sponging the girls' faces, crooning to them as she did so.

"What's that song you're singing?" Brian asked.

"Me? Was I singing?" She hadn't been aware she was doing anything.

"Well, maybe not singing. More like humming, sounded good though."

Embarrassed, Bella flushed. "I don't know what it's called. Kathleen, Bridget's sister, used to sing it all the time at the sanctuary. Said it made her feel closer to her ma."

"You have a nice voice," Brian said, before standing and gathering the empty dishes. "Bella, try to get some rest. You won't do them any good if you fall sick too."

"Brian, what happens now?"

He looked her in the eyes but stayed silent.

"Them? Where will they go?" she asked again.

"I wish I knew. I really wish I knew."

CHAPTER 62

BELLA

The next week passed slowly. Mitch and some of the other men had returned to Riverside Springs. Mitch was keen to get back to Shannon, and Bella couldn't blame him. He promised to tell Mrs. Grayson all that had happened and assure her that Bella would catch up with her work when she got home. She didn't think the older woman would mind her staying with the twins.

Brian stayed, despite Bella telling him to go home to look after his farm.

"I want to stay here. You need someone to

make sure you eat. I don't trust you to look after yourself," Brian said firmly.

While part of her was frustrated to be treated like a child, the other part loved the fact he was so protective. It meant he truly cared about her.

Reverend Franklin and Geoff Rees also stayed.

Gracie and Bella shared the task of looking after the twins. The other children rescued from the farm were sent to Green River where the nuns would take them to an orphanage. But neither Bella or Gracie would let the twins go. Eileen wasn't well enough to travel, and Megan wasn't going anywhere without her twin.

They worked in shifts, so it meant one of them was there the whole time. Gracie told the girls all sorts of fascinating stories. Megan repeated them back to Bella when it was her turn to sit with them.

Finally, at the end of the week, the doctor visited again. He expressed amazement and pronounced Eileen was out of danger. "She will need careful nursing to build up her strength, but in six months she should be as fit as her sister. If you ladies ever want to work as nurses, come find me."

Bella and Gracie exchanged a quick laugh. Relieved, they left the girls sleeping for once and went to join the men. While they had been watching the twins, the circuit judge had arrived.

"He came rather quickly, didn't he?" Bella said.

"Yes, he did," Gracie agreed. "The brothers have a long track record. None of it pretty. Seems they've been in and out of trouble since they were about as young as the twins."

"What will happen to them?" Bella asked.

"Given the evidence, I'm certain they'll hang. The only doubt is whether Rebecca will join them. The judge may be lenient in light of the fact she is a woman, but he's not known for his kindness."

"What of their partners? They couldn't

have done this alone. For one thing, at the very least, the sheriff turned a blind eye. He threatened Gracie when her husband tried to intervene. He should be punished," Bella insisted.

"He will be tried too, Miss Jones. And a couple of other men Rebecca gave up when questioned. I don't think he will have an easy time of it at the penitentiary. Not when they find out he was once a lawman."

Bella didn't care. She had no sympathy for Slater. If he had done the job he was paid to do, the children would have been protected.

"So, what happens now? Do we have to stay for the trial?"

"The judge wants to speak to you, Miss Jones. And to the girls."

"Me? Why?"

"Because you were here when the girls arrived in Mud Butte. You know what they said to Carl Watson. The judge wanted to know why anyone would have left children in the brothers' care."

"Carl couldn't have known what they were like." Bella defended her friend quickly.

"But you had your suspicions."

Bella nodded.

"So why didn't he see the same things?" Sheriff Williams asked.

Bella didn't want to answer but everyone was staring at her.

"Susan, the young girl, reminded me of what I used to be like. I once lived in a similar environment," Bella said, her gaze fixed on the floor. She waited for them to condemn her, but nobody said a word. Brian stepped forward and took her hand.

"If it hadn't been for Gracie writing and Bella refusing to forget those girls, I dread to think how many children would have suffered at the hands of those men," Brian said, squeezing Bella's hand. She returned the squeeze, thankful he had stepped in. She'd been far too embarrassed to continue talking.

"Very true," Reverend Franklin said. "Now,

I must get back to Riverside Springs. Is anyone coming or are you going to stay for the trial?"

The question was addressed toward Brian and Geoff Rees.

"I am going to stay. I want to be sure those varmints are dealt with properly," Brian said. "Once it is over, I will escort Bella back to Riverside Springs."

CHAPTER 63

BELLA

*G*racie and Giles offered Bella and the twins a place to stay while they remained in Mud Butte. Brian and Geoff would stay in town but promised to visit regularly. Everyone felt the twins would be better off being sheltered from the publicity surrounding the trial.

A knock on the bedroom door woke Bella who had dozed off beside Megan. She walked quietly to the door trying not to wake the children. She gasped when she saw her friend standing there, then she was quickly gathered into a hug.

"Bridget, what are you doing here?" Bella asked, finding her voice.

"Brian sent for us," Bridget said, giving her a final squeeze before letting Bella go. "We came as soon as we could. Bella, how could this happen? We thought we were so careful. How are the girls?"

"Doing much better. They don't say much, but the Doc says Eileen is now out of danger."

Bella put her hand on her lips to shush Bridget in case they woke the children. She watched as Bridget silently examined each child, her face turning whiter.

Then they left the room, leaving the door ajar.

"Bella, those injuries. They have been so ill-treated. I can't believe you and Carl met the people who did this."

"I tried to warn him, but he wouldn't listen," Bella said, thinking Bridget was blaming her.

"Bella, nobody is holding you responsible. Carl told me you weren't happy, but he thought," Bridget faltered, her eyes filled with pity and understanding, "your past experiences may have been influencing you. I am so sorry we didn't listen to you, Bella. We should have known better."

"The fault lies with these horrible men. And the townspeople. They should have known something was wrong. But they didn't care enough about the orphans to find out. Why would anyone ignore the plight of the children?"

"Many people believe the children are responsible for their own situation."

"Why would anyone choose to live in poverty and be ill-treated?" Bella asked.

"Bella, we can't lose hope. We have to think of cases like Sally, and Jacob and his sister Lizzie. Those children have found wonderful homes. So have Annie and Liam, you saw that for yourself."

"There's plenty in town who blame Susan

for killing that woman. They don't seem to question what the couple put that girl through."

Bridget wiped a tear away. Bella asked her if she would like some coffee.

"Gracie is in town. She went to see what the latest is on the court case. I won't leave the girls."

Bridget sent her a questioning look.

"I know they will be housed with someone and I am too young to take them, but I need to be with them while I can. You understand that, don't you?"

"Yes, Bella. I do."

Bridget took a seat while Bella made more coffee. She poured it for both of them.

"Geoff Rees has been a godsend," Bella said. "It's not just the fact he seems to know a lot of people, but he has money to pay the bills. I don't think we would have gotten this far without him."

"He is a good man and a wonderful father. Maybe he would take the twins?" Bridget suggested.

"I don't think so. He talks a lot about Liam and Annie and what a lovely family he has. But I doubt he's even thought of extending it."

Bridget stirred her coffee.

"How many times does a child have to suffer before those in New York realize the orphan trains aren't the answer?"

"Bella, I know you went through a horrible time and so did the twins, but the majority of placements appear to work out fine."

"Really?" Bella knew she was being sarcastic, but she was just so angry. Not at Bridget, but at the world. Megan was a totally different child to the outgoing, full of fun girl she had been on the train. Now she jumped at the slightest noise.

"Carl and myself aim to make a difference," Bridget said. "We want to change the way the children are viewed and treated. We got it wrong this time but, unfortunately, we only learn by our mistakes."

Bella didn't know what to say.

"We will continue to make mistakes. We

know every child is not going to be adopted, some people do not want that. The aim of the Children's Aid Society was to provide homes. It was a form of indenture meaning the children work in return for food and lodgings."

Bella was about to protest.

"I know that's not what we dream of, but it is better than the reality of the children living on the streets of New York. We only fail when those we place end up worse off, like these poor kids."

Bella couldn't disagree with Bridget's logic even if it fell far short of the ideal situation.

CHAPTER 64

BELLA

The trial began two days after Bridget and Carl arrived. Bella didn't attend. She couldn't bear to hear what the children had been through and someone had to stay with the girls. Gracie was called as a witness, but Brian stayed with Bella, so she wasn't alone. She enjoyed his company and so did the girls. He didn't make them come sit on his knee or touch them in any way. He let them come to him if they wanted to. At first, they kept their distance, but he continued to play ball with them outside. He also taught them how to look after the animals the MacDonaghs owned. He laughed at Bella's attempts to milk the cow.

"If you think you can do it better, you try," she protested when he kept laughing. She got up so quickly the milk bucket and stool she'd been sitting on overturned. The twins started laughing, causing Bella to stare at them. It was the first time they had laughed since they'd been rescued.

Brian took her elbow and sat her on the stool. He put his hands over hers and gently guided her on how to milk the cow. She couldn't listen to his explanation as her brain was trying not to react to his touch, his nearness, his smell. She didn't fear him like she did most men. In fact, he made her feel safe.

She mastered the art of milking far too quickly for her liking. He praised her efforts before calling to the twins to help him collect the eggs. The twins followed him around like chicks after their mother hen. Watching them, Bella began to have hope for the future.

A rider coming to the house had Brian

reach for his gun. "Bella, take the girls inside. Shut the door and don't come out until I say."

Bella didn't argue. She grabbed both girls and ran to the house. She held them both as they listened to what was happening outside.

"Howdy, stranger. Might I get a drink?" the strange man asked.

"Sure, the well is over there."

"Mind if I rest my horse? I've been riding some ways."

"Sorry, mister," Brian said. "My missus don't like strangers. Take a drink but keep your hands where I can see them."

Bella held her breath wondering what would happen next. Another voice joined in. Thankfully, she recognized Sheriff Williams straight away.

"Hank, what did I tell you about riding up to these people and not introducing yourself. Everyone is on edge. Sorry, Brian, I don't employ him for his brains. He is a great shot though. I came to escort Miss Jones into town," Sheriff Williams said.

"Bella? What do you want with her?"

Bella thought her heart would come right through her chest. Megan held her hand tightly while Eileen pushed the hair back from her forehead. The twins could sense her fear, but she couldn't control it.

"Judge wants a word with her. Don't worry, we'll keep her safe. I promise."

"I want to come with you," Brian said.

Bella had come out of the house by this time. "Brian, you can't. You have to stay here with the girls. We can't leave them alone and we don't want them in town."

"Judge wants to speak to the girls too, but he says he'll come out here and speak to them in private."

"Will he let me stay with them?" Bella asked.

"Probably, Miss Jones. I think that's why he wants you in court today. So nobody can say your evidence is tainted."

"Bella, I don't want you to go into that court alone."

"Thank you, Brian, but I need you to be with the girls. I trust you with them. Please. Look at them, they're scared."

Brian looked at them quickly before turning his attention back to her. "I will be thinking of you. Don't ride back alone. Make sure Geoff or Giles is with you. Understand?"

"Yes, boss," she joked, trying to make light of the situation and hide the fact she was terrified.

He pulled her into his arms and kissed the top of her head. "Hold your head up and tell the truth. I love you," he whispered. "And remember, you're not alone anymore."

She sniffed, trying not to cry.

Sheriff Williams coughed and apologized, "Sorry, Miss Jones, but we didn't think to take a wagon and the MacDonaghs have theirs in town. You will have to ride with me."

"She can have my horse. Samson knows Bella and will mind her."

Brian helped her to mount the horse. She was thankful he had started teaching her to ride while they were waiting for the train. At least she wasn't a complete novice anymore.

"Sheriff, take it easy going back to town. Miss Jones isn't up to a gallop just yet."

"Understood. Miss Jones will set the pace. Good day, Brian, girls."

"Bella, you will come back, won't you?" Megan's fearful comment made her stomach clench.

"I will and, what's more, I will bring you home some candy. You look after Brian and don't let him drink too much coffee," Bella told her.

Megan and Eileen stood holding Brian's hands as Bella rode out. She looked back at them once before facing front. She hoped she would do well in court but couldn't help wishing she had Kathleen by her side. She didn't even know where her friend was.

CHAPTER 65

BELLA

*B*ella dismounted outside the church which was being used as a court house. She let one of the boys standing outside the church look after the horse and followed the sheriff into the court room. She didn't see anyone she knew; her gaze was focused on the judge.

A clerk advised the judge she had arrived. He motioned for her to come forward. The crowd murmured as she walked up to the top of the church. The judge banged his gavel, making her jump.

"Quiet. Court is in session," he roared.

The clerk came forward with the bible and asked her to swear to tell the truth.

She stood with her legs resting at the edge of the chair, holding her hands together tightly trying to quell her nerves.

"Miss Jones, can you please explain to the court how you came to know the twins?" Mr. Perry, the defense attorney asked.

Bella explained how Megan and her sister had come to the sanctuary and how Lily had promised their father they would find them a good home.

"Why were you living in a women's sanctuary, Miss Jones?"

Bella couldn't speak, her mouth was too dry. She looked to the judge, but he didn't offer her any hope. The attorney repeated the question.

"I asked you why you were living in this establishment which I take it caters for fallen women. Are you a fallen woman, Miss Jones?"

"Miss Jones is barely more than a child

herself, Your Honor," the prosecution attorney argued back. "I fail to see what this line of questioning will achieve."

"It goes toward her credibility, Your Honor," Mr. Perry answered. "My clients are fighting for their lives."

"I will allow it," the judge said. "Miss Jones, please answer the question."

"Miss Lily gave me a home when I returned to New York," Bella said.

"But why go to live with this Lily person? Why didn't you go to your own family?" the defense attorney queried.

"I don't have one," she spoke softly.

"Speak up, girl. So, you are an orphan too?" The defense made being an orphan sound like a horrible crime. She shrank farther back almost falling into the chair behind her.

"Yes, sir."

He looked to the judge then to the crowd watching before turning his attention back to her. It seemed everyone was waiting to hear what he asked next.

"So, why didn't you go to an orphanage?" Mr. Perry's tone suggested that was the smart option.

Bella's legs started to shake. She looked around the room in desperation, but nobody came to her aid. She realized, on some level, they couldn't, but it didn't stop the sweat running down her back. She bit her lip continuously.

"Miss Jones?"

"I didn't want to be put on the orphan train again," she said, finally.

"So, you admit you were a runaway?" Mr. Perry smiled but it didn't warm up his eyes. He hesitated before saying loudly, "Perhaps also a criminal?"

"I didn't do anything wrong," Bella insisted quietly.

"Didn't you? Then why did you end up back in New York. The orphan train people found you a place to live, didn't they? A new family." The defense attorney seemed to answer his own question, but when she didn't reply, he looked at her, his eyes piercing hers.

Bella nodded.

"So why run away?"

"They didn't treat me right," she replied, wishing her voice would stop shaking.

"They didn't buy you nice clothes, you mean?" Mr. Perry sneered.

"No, it wasn't like that. The woman, she beat me all the time," she protested, her voice rising slightly.

"Maybe she had just cause to beat you. Children need discipline. Just as my clients had to discipline the children in their care."

"That wasn't discipline. Nobody needs to be hurt like that," she retorted sharply.

"Like what?" Mr. Perry asked.

Bella stared at the attorney. She believed he could see right through her, read what was in her head. She couldn't admit to that in public. If she did, she would be ruined forever. But if she didn't, then maybe these terrible men would be set free. She was trapped, the room seemed to be getting smaller, there was no air. She opened her mouth but couldn't speak, her lips and tongue were too dry. She heard a chair scraping back as someone stood.

"Your Honor, may I please speak?"

Bella recognized Bridget's voice, but it seemed like it was coming from a great distance. The defense attorney protested but the Judge said he would allow it.

"My name is Bridget Watson. I lived in the sanctuary with Bella and some other girls. Lily Doherty, the owner, provided us with a home in return for our labor."

"So, are you a runaway too?" the defense attorney sneered. Bella gripped the side of her chair. She didn't want Bridget to lose her temper and get into trouble. The Judge could throw her in jail for contempt.

"No, sir!" Bridget replied, but nobody was left in any doubt by the use of her tone, the sir wasn't meant to be complimentary.

"Your Honor, I moved to the sanctuary of my own free will. Believe me, when I say

Bella Jones is a young lady of the highest integrity."

"Thank you, Mrs. Watson, but the question remains. Why did you run out on your adoptive family, Miss Jones?" the Judge asked Bella. His eyes seemed kinder than the defense attorney, almost as if he was willing to listen without judging her first.

She had to say something. Megan and Eileen were depending on her.

"They didn't treat me right. They beat me, starved me, and when I started getting older, the man he... he..." She looked helplessly at the judge.

"He what, Miss Jones?" The defense attorney demanded an answer.

"That's enough," the Judge intervened. "I think we all can imagine what happened to this unfortunate young lady."

The crowd started whispering and staring at her. They were judging her. Just like everyone else had. Just like she had. They were blaming her. She stood straighter.

"I was ten years old," Bella said. "Same age as Susan."

At first the crowd kept talking, but gradually everyone stopped to listen to what she said.

"I didn't know what was happening or why, but I knew it was wrong. That's why I ran, and that's why I knew leaving the twins with those men was a mistake." She pointed at Joe and Jack before turning to face the judge. "I can't tell you why, sir, I mean, Your Honor, but I just get a feeling when I am near men who would treat children that way."

"Thank you, Miss Jones," the judge said. "You are excused."

"I haven't finished my questions, Your Honor. She left the twins with my clients. If she believed those children to be at risk, she is guilty too."

"I didn't have a choice. I didn't want to leave the children, but nobody would listen to me. I don't have any money, and I am not even a grown woman. I have no voice, just like the twins and Susan and the other children your clients, and men like them, prey on. I had no choice; do you hear me? And because of that, the children I promised to look after will bear the scars of their abuse for years to come."

The court erupted. People were talking at once, the judge banging his gavel, but nobody paid him any attention. Bella fell back into the chair, tears running down her face. Bridget pushed through the crowd with Gracie following right behind her. Both women put their arms around Bella.

"You were wonderful," Bridget exclaimed, giving her a hanky to dry her eyes.

"You are such a strong woman, Bella," Gracie said. "I am proud to have you as my friend."

"But I made things worse. Look, everyone is arguing."

It was true, the noise level in the church was unbelievable with what appeared to be everyone talking at once.

"You opened their eyes, Bella," Bridget assured her. "You gave mistreated children a voice. Now, come on. Let's get you out of here."

"But what about the judge?"

"Miss Jones, thank you for coming today. You were very brave. I apologize for what happened to you when you were a child and should have been protected. I will pray you learn to forgive yourself because, believe me, you played no part in what happened to you or these other children." The Judge took a deep breath. "I think you should take a seat. I don't think you will want to miss the next bit."

Bridget and Gracie escorted Bella down to a seat in the front row. They sat on either side of her, each holding one of her hands. The judge roared at the crowd and banged the gavel several times more until the room fell quiet.

"I have heard enough over the past week of this trial. There is no doubt in my mind that these men are guilty as charged. I believe they should both hang for their crimes."

The gavel came down again as the noise level increased once more.

"Silence," the judge ordered. "I haven't finished. I also sentence Rebecca Kingston/Maitland to twenty years hard labor. Madam, you deserve to hang but a small part of my mind believes the story you gave me. That you acted out of fear of your husband. Also, I am mindful that you have provided Sheriff Williams with the names of the other men involved in this despicable circle of abuse. I intend to ensure each and every one of those men are tried and punished for their crimes. Starting tomorrow with Sheriff Slater who is lucky not to be sharing the fate of his friends. I wish to give thanks to all who bore witness at this trial, in particular to Mrs. Gracie MacDonagh whose brave actions started the rescue of these children. And to Miss Jones who, despite her own sorrowful experiences, has let nothing stand in her way in her efforts to protect these children. Finally, I am hopeful Mud Butte and its occupants have learned from this awful experience. Every child matters, regardless of color, race, or creed. Court is dismissed."

The people cheered for the judge, but Bella couldn't do or say anything. It was like all the fight had left her body. She hoped people would listen to the wise old judge, but in her experience, words were easily forgotten. Bridget helped her to her feet.

"Let's go back and tell Brian. Then we can prepare to go home," Bridget said, casting a glance at Bella. Mortified the tears kept falling, Bella nodded to the judge and allowed Bridget and Gracie to escort her out of the court room. Sheriff Williams ushered them out a back door.

CHAPTER 66

BELLA

After the trial, everyone gathered back in the MacDonaghs' house, although it was a tight squeeze. Gracie insisted Bella stay seated. Bridget obviously had filled Brian in about what happened in town as he refused to leave her side.

"When do we leave for Riverside Springs?" Carl asked.

"As soon as we can. No offense, but I can't wait to put the town of Mud Butte behind me," Brian said, holding Bella's hand under the table.

Bella didn't say anything. She didn't know what was going to happen to the twins.

"Amen," Carl added. "And you, Mr. and Mrs. MacDonagh, what will you do?"

Gracie gave her husband a quick look before she said, "We're selling our house. It doesn't feel right staying in Mud Butte. Wasn't just the sheriff who turned a blind eye to what was happening to the children."

"Are you still going to Green River?" Bella asked, wondering if they were going to volunteer to adopt the twins now. Financially, it would be a struggle, yet she couldn't see how Gracie could turn her back on the girls. It was obvious that she loved them. Bella did too but nobody was going to let a single woman adopt a baby let alone six-year-old twins.

Gracie didn't answer her but looked at her husband, a stricken look on her face. His expression was grave.

Mr. Rees broke the silence.

"Giles, Gracie, I've been thinking. I have a

small homestead—it's barely more than one room at the moment—on the edge of my property. I wondered if you would be interested in it."

A spark of hope lit up Gracie's face, making her careworn face look pretty.

"We don't have any money," Giles replied, staring at his shoes.

"I don't want to sell it, well at least not right now. I thought we could do a deal. If you farm the land around it, we can split the profits. Then in five years' time, if you wish to buy the land and the house, you can."

Gracie stared at Geoff, an expression of disbelief on her face.

"Why would you do something like that for us?" she asked him.

"I have been lucky in my life, Gracie. I was born into a loving family who worked hard and provided us with the best education. I married a wonderful woman and now have been blessed with two children thanks to the orphan train. Megan and Eileen need love, lots of it, to help them get over their ordeal. I think you and Giles can provide that."

Bella stared at Gracie. The woman was completely bowled over by Geoff's generosity.

"I am not sure we can accept such a generous gift, Mr. Rees."

Gracie's face fell at her husband's words

"I know you have your pride, Giles. You're a hardworking, decent man. But please, let me help you. You will be helping me as well as the other residents in Riverside Springs. Our town needs more people, couples like you and Gracie. And my children need friends."

"You mean, you would allow us to have the girls?" Giles asked, his voice filled with doubt.

Carl nodded. "Assuming you want the two of them. They can't be parted, especially after everything they have been through."

"Oh yes, both of them. We couldn't choose between them either," Gracie said quietly. "I think they would be more comfortable living in

Riverside Springs with people they know. And it would mean they don't have to say goodbye to Bella." She stared at her husband, her eyes pleading with him.

Bella willed the man to say yes. She couldn't bear having to say goodbye to the girls, not again. She would also miss Gracie who had become such a good friend.

"I guess we could accept if you agreed to some sort of payment schedule," Mr. Mac-Donagh said, taking Gracie's hand in his. "We both want a family. We will love those girls like our own."

"We will, I promise you, Mr. Rees," Gracie added.

"I believe you, Gracie. Carolyn, my wife, will be thrilled to have some female company nearby. She gets a mite tired of listening to me and Brian discussing man stuff, doesn't she, Brian?"

"She is a lovely woman. Can you guys please excuse us. Bella and myself need to have a talk," Brian said, taking Bella by the hand and almost pulling her out of the door.

Bella's stomach roiled. Had he changed his mind about her?

CHAPTER 67

BELLA

*B*rian held Bella's hand as they walked a bit past the barn. The twins waved to them, they were playing with Shep, the dog, who had quickly become devoted to the girls.

"Bella, I know today was really difficult for you. And I also know you would love to give those girls a home, but..."

"I'm too young," she said, before he could go on.

"You would make a wonderful mother in time. But for now, I think you need to take some time to let yourself be happy. As far as I can see, you've spent a long time running from your past and looking over your shoulder."

Bella shrugged. She didn't want to dredge up the past again.

"I want you to know I aim to marry you, Bella. When you are of age. But I want everyone to know we have an understanding. I don't want to risk you running off with some cowboy."

She giggled at his expression as he tried to look fierce. Then she stopped giggling. "I wouldn't do that, Brian. Not to you."

"So, will you marry me, when you are eighteen?"

"I would, but…"

"But?" His face fell.

"I don't know when my birthday is. My ma didn't leave a note when she left me. All I know is she was an actress and her new fella didn't want any babies around. That's what I was told."

"Oh, Bella, she was a fool to leave you. I

will never do that. So, you could be eighteen already?"

Bella nodded shyly.

Brian let out a whoop before he pulled her into his arms and kissed her gently. His lips grazed hers just like a butterfly.

"When we get back to Riverside Springs, let's speak to Reverend Franklin. He will know what to do."

She nodded.

He kissed her lightly again before leading her back into the house.

CHAPTER 68

KATHLEEN

athleen didn't visit her brothers again. The trial opened the next day. She dressed carefully, wanting the jury to see the boys came from a good family. Richard had bought her brothers new suits for the court case. Michael kept pulling at the collar of his shirt as if it were too small for him, but Shane looked very handsome and terrified.

The judge was grumpy, and from the start it was clear he had no sympathy for the boys. When Randolph suggested the tragic loss of their parents, their youth, their arrival on the orphan train and subsequent ill-treatment were the cause of their actions, the judge disagreed.

"They are old enough to know better. Seems they were in trouble before they left New York. Those orphan trains are the bane of society. All they do is move the New York criminals out to decent towns like ours."

Kathleen couldn't believe her ears. She had heard similar comments, of course, but not usually from educated men like a judge. She opened her mouth, but Richard placed his hand on her arm, warning her not to say a word. She could be put in jail too.

Various witnesses came forward, each one making things worse. All the men swore Beaugrand was a wonderful boss and would never get involved in anything dodgy. They didn't know of any argument with Diaz. They also complimented the man who had employed the boys. Older orphans, who seemingly used to work for the same man on that ranch, came forward claiming to have been treated like family with regular meals and schooling.

"Seems like he was a regular saint, the man who took the boys in. He must have been taking orphans from the first day those trains arrived in Freesburg," Richard whispered.

Kathleen looked at him then back at the men. Of course, they weren't all orphans, but men paid to testify. Why couldn't anyone else see that? But the jury were nodding their heads in agreement as the prosecution made out orphans to be criminals purely because they were orphans.

Kathleen fidgeted in her seat, wishing Bridget or Lily were there. If they got up to speak, people would listen to them. But nobody cared about her brothers. They didn't want to know that the only reason they had been in prison in New York was because of a personal vendetta. She itched to tell the truth, but the judge refused her pleas to testify, claiming she had nothing of value to say.

CHAPTER 69

KATHLEEN

*R*ichard was called to the stand and testified to the condition of the two men. Mr Lait, the prosecutor, tried to twist Richard's words to make it sound like the injuries the boys had received were their own fault.

"They didn't beat themselves up, and Michael certainly didn't break his own arm," Richard argued. "As I said, their injuries are consistent with their story. They both bear marks of sustained ongoing abuse. This proves their story of neglect at the hands of the ranch owner is true."

"Doctor Green, you came to know these boys because of their sister, Kathleen Collins, didn't you?" Mr. Lait asked. The prosecution attorney had a way of making everything sound sordid.

"I don't think that is relevant."

"So, you don't think the fact that you are in love with their sister prejudices you in any way." Mr Lait sneered before turning to look directly at Kathleen. "I mean, I can see why, she is a beauty, isn't she?"

Kathleen wanted to crawl under the seat in front of her as all eyes turned to look at her. Michael scowled, making him look even guiltier.

"Sir, I demand you stop this line of questioning. Miss Collins was working as an agent for a children's charity when I met her," Richard protested.

"Yes, a child in her care was injured in a fire. Trouble seems to follow this family around, wouldn't you say, Doctor?" Mr. Lait replied.

The question was rhetorical as the prosecutor sat before Richard got a chance to answer.

The judge called a halt to the proceedings, telling everyone to come back the next day.

"That went well today, didn't it?" Kathleen said, not hiding her sarcasm as they were leaving the court. Her brothers had been taken away in shackles and she was smarting from the abuse they had taken. How dare these people look down on them because they were orphans. They hadn't killed their parents.

"Miss Collins, don't lose hope," Mr. James said. "It is early days yet. Any news from your Pinkertons, Green?"

"Not yet," Richard said. "He'll come through with something."

"You should give up and go home. Nobody is going to say a bad word about me."

Kathleen swung around at the smug voice.

She wanted to wipe the smile from his conceited face, but that's what he wanted.

"Beaugrand, what are you doing here? You shouldn't be talking to us. You're on the stand tomorrow," Richard said.

"Just wanted to see how you were doing, pretty lady," Beaugrand said, smiling a crooked smile. "Always room in my employment for a lady like yourself."

"Oh you—" Kathleen fired back, but Richard put his arm around her waist, stopping her from taking a step nearer Beaugrand.

"Come on, Miss Collins, let's get you home."

Kathleen let Richard lead her away. He let go of her waist, holding onto her arm instead.

"Thank you," she said, once her temper had cooled a bit.

"I wish you could have smacked him, but you would have only played into his hands," Richard said. "I never guessed you had such a temper."

"I don't usually. But that man, he just gets

under my skin. He is lower than a rattlesnake's belly."

Richard laughed. "Of that there is no doubt. Now, let's have some dinner. Mr. James, are you joining us?"

"No, thank you, Richard. I have to prepare for tomorrow."

"I can't eat either, but thank you for the invitation," Kathleen declined.

"You must eat. And you cannot look like you are beaten," Richard insisted. "Think of this trial like a game of poker. You cannot show Beaugrand your hand."

Poker? Her brothers' lives were at risk and he was telling her to play cards.

"Really, Doctor Green," she remonstrated.

"Yes, really, Miss Collins," he countered, leaving her speechless.

CHAPTER 70

KATHLEEN

The next day was worse. Beaugrand, looking like a well-to-do banker rather than a self-made rancher, took the stand and swore on the bible to tell the truth, then promptly lied his way through the next few hours. To Kathleen, it was obvious he was lying. His eyes roved around the room, and he wouldn't look at anyone straight in the face. But the jury seemed dazzled by his wealth and his clothes. He swore he was nowhere near Freesburg when the man was killed.

"But what do you make of the fact that the defense can produce witnesses stating you were there?" Mr. Lait asked.

"Who are these men? Poor laborers and ranch hands. All scraping around for their next dollar."

Kathleen couldn't believe his nerve. She glanced at the jury, surely, they could see he was lying but they seemed to be swallowing every word that came out of his mouth.

"Don't let the jury see your fear. They are watching you," Richard coached her quietly. She sat straighter. She was terrified, but she wasn't about to let anyone see it.

Midway through the afternoon, the prosecution called for the trial to end.

"Your Honor, the defense has provided no evidence to prove their innocence," the prosecutor said. "Everything points to their guilt. What are we waiting for? String them up and let us all go home."

"Mr. Lait, this is my court room. Why don't you do your job, and let me do mine?"

Kathleen almost cheered. This was the first indication the judge was annoyed with the prosecution. But the attorney had a point. They didn't have any more witnesses.

The door to the back of the court opened and a man came in. Richard stood and whispered something to Mr. James.

"If it pleases Your Honor, I request a short break," Mr. James said. "Some valuable information has come to my attention."

"What information? This is another delaying tactic on the part of the defense," Lait protested.

"I assure you, it isn't. We listened to your witness all morning. Please allow me twenty minutes."

"You have fifteen, and not a second longer." The judge hit the gavel. The noise in the court room rose considerably, but Kathleen's attention was pinned to the new arrival. Mr. James ushered them all into a small meeting room and closed the door.

"Mr. James, Miss Collins, this is Mr. Meredith, a Pinkerton agent."

"What did you find out?" Richard asked the man.

"Beaugrand isn't his real name," Mr. Meredith said, wasting no time. "It's Mac-Arthur, and he is a wanted man in the United Kingdom. Seems he murdered some duke and escaped with cash and jewelry worth a hundred thousand dollars."

"How do you know it is him? That's a pretty big claim, isn't it?" Mr. James asked.

"I have proof. That's what took me so long. I had to find the woman who helped him. She is in a boarding house on the edge of town. Didn't want to risk bringing her in here," Mr. Meredith replied.

"We need more than the word of a woman," Mr James retorted, before seeming to remember Kathleen was present. "No offense, Miss Collins, but you have seen the judge. He isn't going to believe a woman over a man."

"No, but he will believe this. I have also

wired London and they are sending their people over. It will take them time to get here, but I think the judge will agree it is in his interest to cooperate," Mr. Meredith said.

Kathleen couldn't believe what she was hearing.

"And if that wasn't enough, MacArthur's killing spree didn't end on the other side of the pond. He is also wanted in Boston. Quite an interesting trail he left, once you know where to start digging."

"Anything to pin him to this murder?" Richard asked.

The Pinkerton detective looked Richard straight in the eye. "No, but given he is the prosecution's star witness, it is enough to cast doubt on his testimony. That should help, shouldn't it?'

"I don't know," Richard said. "Mr. James?"

"We will soon find out. We best get back in there, or the judge will convict just to show us he is in charge."

"He has to allow the jury to reach a verdict," Kathleen protested.

"Do you think that will take long?" Mr. James retorted before ushering them back into the court room.

CHAPTER 71

KATHLEEN

"Mr. James are you ready to proceed?"

"Yes, Your Honor. We call Mr. Beaugrand back to the stand," Mr. James responded in a very respectful but calm tone.

"Your Honor, I think we have heard everything Mr. Beaugrand has to say." Mr. Lait stood, his contemptuous tone matched by the look he sent Mr. James.

"No doubt, but I am sure Mr. Beaugrand would be happy to speak to us again." The judge's sarcasm made the audience laugh.

Kathleen kept her eyes on Beaugrand; she saw his frustration and perhaps a little bit of fear before the mask appeared. He walked to the witness stand and sat once more.

"Mr. Beaugrand, I remind you, you are under oath," Mr. James said.

"Yes, sir, but I am not on trial here. I'm no orphan." The jury smiled in response.

"I don't know whether you are or not, but I do know your name isn't Beaugrand, is it?"

The courtroom erupted as people spoke at once.

"Quiet. Quiet." The judge banged his gavel. Beaugrand was on his feet protesting too, but the judge told him to sit down and shut up. "Mr. James, I trust you have reason to make those assertations."

"Yes, Your Honor. This man isn't an American citizen, but a British one. The name the British authorities know him as is Robert Mac-Arthur, but, of course, that may also be false. He is wanted for murder and theft to the tune of a hundred thousand dollars."

"This is ridiculous. How dare you? My name is Beaugrand."

Mr. James ignored Beaugrand. "We have a witness, Your Honor, who can identify him. We also have a wire from London confirming the information."

"She can't tell you anything," Beaugrand blustered. "For a few dollars she would claim the judge was the King of England."

"Your Honor, you will note I didn't qualify the sex of the witness," Mr. James said lightly.

The judge gave Beaugrand a shrewd look before turning back to Mr. James. "Give me those papers. Who gave them to you?"

"We engaged the services of a Pinkerton agent, Your Honor."

"After the homestead massacre, nobody pays any attention to those people anymore." Beaugrand huffed.

"My son is a Pinkerton agent, Mr. Beaugrand." The judge's response left nobody in any doubt of his opinion of the man in front of him. "Guard, take Beaugrand, or

Macarthur or whatever his name is, into custody until I hear what the Pinkerton agent has to say."

Beaugrand protested loudly but nobody paid any attention to him as the guard took him away.

The judge instructed the Pinkerton agent to come forward and had him swear on the Bible. "Do you know my son?"

"Yes, Your Honor. I've had the pleasure to work with him on a couple of cases."

"Very good. Now tell us what you know."

Kathleen listened with only half an ear, she didn't really care what Beaugrand had done. Instead, she watched the jury, wondering if what they were hearing was enough to get her brothers released.

"And this lady is willing to come and swear the truth?" the judge asked.

"Yes, Your Honor, but she is afraid of Mac-Arthur, he has threatened her."

"I can imagine," the judge said. "I think I have heard enough."

The judge thanked the Pinkerton agent for his service then focused on the jury.

"You must disregard everything the man, Beaugrand, has told you. It appears he is at best a con artist, at worst a multiple murderer. With regard to the men on trial, it would appear there is insufficient evidence available to convict them of murder. They may very well be innocent of that crime. I therefore dismiss the jury, with thanks for their service."

Kathleen's hopes soared as she jumped to her feet. Her brothers would be free, and they could all travel to Riverside Springs together.

"However, these men are, by their own admission, cattle rustlers and that would usually mean a hanging offence," the judge went on.

Kathleen sat suddenly. She couldn't believe it. He was still going to hang her brothers.

"Given their relative youth, the circumstances of their arrival in our state, and the mistreatment they have already endured, I am sentencing them to five years in State penitentiary.

The court erupted once more, the judge banged his gavel. "Bailiffs, clear the court. Take the prisoners to the cells."

KATHLEEN COULDN'T MOVE. The tears rolled down her face and she didn't bother to hide them. Richard pulled her to her feet and escorted her from the court house. Reporters jostled, trying to get her opinion, but she didn't say a word. Richard called a cab and instructed the driver to take them to Mr. James' house. Only when they got there, and they were safely inside, did he speak.

"I am so sorry, Kathleen," Richard said gently. "I was sure once we got Beaugrand uncovered for what he was, your brothers would be safe."

Kathleen looked at him. What could she say? Her brothers were alive, so she should be thankful to him for saving them. But she couldn't feel anything but anger. Not at him, but at the system that had sent them to this state, that had allowed them to be mistreated. The same system that had failed the other children.

"Kathleen?" Richard queried.

"I best get packed. I have to get back to New York. Then, once I repay you, I shall move to Riverside Springs."

"Repay me?"

"I know it will take a while, but you will get back every penny I owe you." Kathleen didn't even want to think about how long it would take her to repay her debts. All she wanted was to be back in New York with Bridget and Lily.

"You think I care about the money?" Richard said, looking hurt. "Kathleen, I thought you were smarter than that. I care about you."

Kathleen didn't want to hear that. She couldn't deal with anything else today. She stood.

"Thank you for everything, but I really need to pack now. Please excuse me."

And she walked away feeling his eyes staring at the back of her head.

CHAPTER 72

KATHLEEN

Kathleen looked at her packed bag. She hadn't slept a wink last night. How was she going to tell Bridget the news? She left the bag on the bed and went to check at the train station for the next train to New York.

She hadn't gone far down the street when she heard someone calling her name. Turning, she found Richard.

"We've got to go to the court house," he told her.

She turned back in the direction of the train station. "I am going to New York."

"No, Kathleen. Judge wants to see us. All of us."

"Why?" she asked.

"I have no idea, but it must be important. It can't be more bad news, can it?"

Kathleen looked into his earnest eyes, willing herself to believe him. But she couldn't deal with anything else. She was barely holding it together.

"Come on. You can get a later train," he said.

She covered her ears as he whistled for a cab.

"Sorry, old habit," he said, taking her hand.

She smiled at him. The cab driver drove fast to the court house in response to the big tip Richard had promised. Walking in the door, Kathleen took a deep breath.

There were only the judge, Mr. James, Mr. Lait, and the sheriff.

"Thank you all for coming. I have had a

chance to speak to the defendants, Shane and Michael Collins. Michael has admitted he was the one solely involved with the cattle rustling. According to him, the younger defendant is totally innocent. Corroborating evidence suggests that this may be the case. No witnesses have mentioned Shane, but they all implicate Michael," the judge explained, directing his remarks to Mr. James.

"What does this mean?" Kathleen asked, causing the judge to glare at her. Richard took her hand and squeezed gently to show his support.

"I have no option but to release Shane. The issue I have is he doesn't wish to return to the home he was placed in. He says he would rather go to prison."

"He can't do that," Kathleen burst out. Again, she apologized.

"What do we need, Your Honor?" Mr. James asked.

"An adult, preferably a responsible one, to accept responsibility for him until he is twenty-one years old. Someone has to teach this young man right from wrong."

Kathleen bristled. The judge knew her brother wasn't guilty of cattle rustling, yet he still wrote him off as being a criminal.

"My sister and brother-in-law live in New York. I can wire them, but it will take time for them to come out to Waterloo. I am not even sure if they are in New York. They work as outplacement agents for the orphan society." At the look on the Judge's face she might as well have announced they were axe murderers.

"I will take responsibility for Shane, Your Honor," Richard said.

"You will? What do you do for a living?" the judge asked, looking surprised.

"I am a doctor and I also hold a few investments."

"Can you afford to keep this man? He must not be tempted to turn to a life of crime." The judge didn't see the amused glances his words caused.

Mr. James coughed as if clearing his throat,

but Kathleen guessed he was trying to cover his amusement.

"Your Honor, Richard Green is a member of the railroad Green family."

Kathleen wanted to laugh at the expression on the judge's face, only his attitude disgusted her. Richard was automatically elevated in his estimation as he was well off.

She looked at the ground as the judge and Richard signed the paperwork. Mr. James witnessed it. The judge didn't ask Kathleen for her input. She realized he hadn't expected her to be there at all, but Richard had brought her of his own will knowing it was important to her.

"Are you ready?" Richard asked once they'd finished.

She had missed some of the conversation and looked at him in puzzlement.

"You have to say goodbye to Michael for now, but we get to take Shane home."

"We?" she asked.

"Well, I guess you're stuck with me for a

while, Miss Collins. I don't intend on letting you travel back to New York alone."

She didn't get a chance to say a word. Michael and Shane were brought into the room. At the judge's direction, Shane was unfettered. He rubbed his arms, his shocked face showing he didn't believe what was happening. Kathleen locked eyes with Michael. She saw the regret in his eyes. She went over to him and wrapped her arms around him, being careful of his arm.

"You are an amazing man," she said.

"He was innocent," her brother insisted.

"I am the queen of England," she whispered back.

Michael gave her a quick look then looked away. "He would never have been able to handle prison."

"Write to me, Michael," she begged him. "When you get out, you have a home with me. Wherever I end up. We are family, and nothing is going to change that."

"Look after him, Kathy," he said. His use

of his old childhood name for her filled her eyes with tears. He looked at her one more time, his eyes flickered to Shane then he was gone.

"Come on, let's get out of here," Richard said.

Kathleen let Richard shepherd her and her brother out of there. They went back to Mr. James' house to pick up her belongings. Richard left the siblings to catch up while he went shopping for some train tickets and some things for Shane.

Soon, they were on the train back to Freesburg to check on Patrick and from there they traveled on to New York.

* * *

"SHANE, would you mind taking a walk through the train. I wish to speak to your sister, please."

"Yes, Doc Richard." Shane stood. They were traveling in first class thanks to Richard's generosity. It was so different from the train journey she had made with Miss Screed.

"Kathleen, I hope you don't mind my impertinence, but I felt we better talk now, while we can. Once you get back to New York, I am sure your sister and friends will monopolize your company."

She tried to smile, but her facial muscles wouldn't respond. Her palms were sweating so she hid them in the folds of her skirt. She couldn't look him in the face, every time she stared into his eyes, her insides seemed to melt.

"I want you to know I admire you, Kathleen," he said formally. She glanced at him and saw he was nervous. His eyelid was twitching ever so slightly.

"What I mean is, do you think you might come to care for me?"

"I do already. You are a very dear friend," she replied hastily, hoping to make him smile.

"A friend? That wasn't quite what I had in mind," he replied. "I see you as much more than a friend. I know there is an age gap between us, but I don't care. I can't imagine my life without you in it."

"You can't?"

"No. I know you have plans to go to Riverside Springs, but I was hoping you might change them. I know that's a lot to ask but I have such a wonderful opportunity at the New York hospital. I want to study plastic surgery. I worked with a lot of burns victims in the past, children like Patrick and adults too. I believe we can do a lot more to help those afflicted. But it will mean more years of training."

She was torn. She wanted to get to know him better, she knew she liked him a lot, but she had plans to go to Riverside Springs. She wanted to live with her family.

"I know I've sprung this on you, but do you think you could consider it. There is a lot of work to be done in New York. We can help children together." He paused, looking at her in the face as he took her hands. "What do you think?"

She longed to say yes but she barely knew

him. He had been wonderful to her on this trip. Without his help she wouldn't be bringing Shane back to New York. But did she love him or feel grateful to him? She didn't know.

"You don't feel the same way I do?" he said softly, his voice trembling slightly. Withdrawing his hands, he moved away from her. "I apologize."

She grabbed his hands in a most unladylike fashion, but she couldn't bear to see him hurting.

"I like you a lot, more than any man I have met. But I don't know if I can live in New York. I miss my siblings and I promised Bella I would go to Riverside Springs." She took a deep breath, "Richard, could you give me some time to consider your request?"

"Yes, of course," he said, pulling her close again, smiling into her eyes.

She saw his gaze move from her eyes to her mouth and back again. Before she knew what was happening, he leant in and brushed his lips against hers. The instant he kissed her, she knew she wanted more. She clung to him as he kissed her again.

Shane's arrival interrupted them.

"Sorry," Shane said, not looking in the least bit apologetic. "So, have you asked her yet?"

"Shane!" Kathleen admonished her brother.

"Yes, I have, Shane, but your sister is a wise woman. She wants us to wait a while to see how she feels once we are all back in New York. I live in hope," Richard said, smiling at Kathleen.

She couldn't control the butterflies in her stomach. Being held in his arms had been so wonderful. Was that what love meant?

"I will wait as long as you want, darling," Richard whispered once Shane was distracted.

She couldn't reply. She wanted to pinch herself to see if what was happening was real.

CHAPTER 73

KATHLEEN

*C*arl had sent a telegram to Kathleen with the address of their New York home. They had rented it to give Bridget some quiet time to recover from her illness. The fact Bridget was staying away from Lily and her new babies as well as the children of the sanctuary made Kathleen fear the worst. She called to the house and barely had Carl opened the door when she was on her way upstairs.

"Bridget, how are you?"

Bridget sat up straighter in the bed. Kathleen tried to hide how worried she was. Her sister was so pale.

"Much better for seeing you. I am so glad you're back," Bridget said. Kathleen leaned in to kiss Bridget on the cheek, feeling for herself how thin her sister was. She hoped she was up to the shock.

"I brought someone with me. Are you up to seeing visitors?"

"Kathleen, I'm in bed," Bridget admonished gently.

"I know that, silly, but Shane has seen you plenty of times," Kathleen said. She waited as Bridget registered what she had said. Her sister's face paled even more as she sat up straighter in bed.

"Shane? He's here? Oh my."

Shane came into the bedroom. He faltered at the sight of Bridget and glanced at Kathleen. She motioned him to sit down.

"Shane. Oh, how good it is to see you." Bridget pulled him close into a hug. Then she looked over his shoulder at the door. "Is Michael with you?"

"No, Bridget. Michael is staying in Iowa for a while," Kathleen replied before quickly changing the subject. Bridget would learn the truth in time. "So, tell us, what did the doctors say?"

"They said I will make a full recovery. I just need to be careful for the next while. I have a heart complaint," Bridget explained, her hand still gripping Shane as if afraid he would disappear.

Kathleen couldn't say a word.

"I'll be fine, Kathleen. Once I take my medication, I am the same as everyone else. I just tire a little easier and have some dizzy spells."

The bedroom door opened, and Carl came in carrying a tray.

"I thought your brother's arrival would put a smile on your face," he said. "Kathleen too. Bridget has missed both of you so much."

"We've missed her, haven't we, Shane?"

Kathleen said. "Isn't it wonderful news about Lily and the babies."

"Imagine, twins and nobody knew," Carl said. "I think poor Charlie got a heart attack, but he's as proud as punch now. Have you seen them yet?"

"We're heading there next. We wanted to see Bridget first."

"Kathleen, there are some letters for you downstairs from Bella. They arrived after you left. I can tell you now, read the latest one first." Bridget sounded tired.

Kathleen nudged Shane and nodded her head toward the door.

"Let's go and see the twins and I can read my letters. We will be back later."

"Yeah, Kathleen has to introduce you to Richard," Shane said, standing up.

"Who's Richard?" Bridget asked, her eyes flickering between Shane and Kathleen. Before Kathleen could answer, Shane did.

"Her fiancé."

"Shane Collins, get out that door before I

474

hit you," Kathleen ordered. "Richard is not my fiancé. He is a wonderful man who I met on the train, he helped me with Patrick. He's staying in New York and will come for dinner soon. Now rest, Bridget. We will chat later."

Shane disappeared before she could get her hands on him. Imagine telling Bridget she was engaged. Carl followed them out of the room.

"How is she really?" she asked Carl once the door closed.

"She will be fine, Kathleen. She gave us all a bit of a fright, but with the right treatment and care she will be as good as new."

Carl was being honest, she could tell that from his facial expression, but she was going to ask Richard to check on Bridget. He might be able to reassure her.

She opened the letters from Bella. The latest one read:

"Dear Kathleen,

I hope by the time you read this letter you will have found your brothers and be back living in New York planning your trip to River-side Springs. I miss you.

This place is everything you thought it would be. It is more than I ever believed it could be. Kathleen, I've fallen in love and, what's more amazing, he is in love with me. Brian Curran, yes, the man who was supposed to marry Bridget, is a farmer and so much more. He is also an orphan train survivor and knows what it was like.

I can't wait for you to meet him. We will be getting married next year. We both want to wait until you are here to be my bridesmaid. Please write back and tell us when you will be coming.

I have lots more news for you but just wanted to get this in the post.

With lots of love

BELLA.

EPILOGUE

Christmas, Riverside Springs, Wyoming

*B*ella glanced up from her machine to see Brian trudging through the snow as he crossed Main Street. He was carrying a Christmas tree. Her stomach leapt as butterflies flew around inside. She had to pinch herself that this fine man had chosen her to be his bride. They had spoken to Reverend Franklin who suggested they take some time to get to know each other properly. Bella knew the pastor was a little worried she had fallen for Brian as she saw him as some sort of rescuer. Perhaps she had at first. But over the last few months, he had proven over and over how wonderful he was.

She picked up her skirt and hurried out to meet him.

"There you are," he greeted her with a smile. "Is this big enough?"

"It's wonderful. I have made some decorations for it," she said as she examined the tree. "Megan and Eileen helped. I told them they can be here when you put the star on the top of the tree."

"A star," he teased, "I thought you would prefer an angel." He stole a kiss before asking, "Where would you like your first Christmas tree, Miss Jones?"

"Right here please, Mr. Curran," she said, her laughter bubbling over.

"I'll make you some popcorn for you to string together," Mrs. Grayson said. "Reverend Franklin asked me to tell you he was looking for you, Brian."

"Thanks. I best leave you two ladies be. You look busy."

"That's the understatement of the year. Bella has so many dresses to finish, I think she will be working right through to Christmas day."

"Don't work too hard, Bella."

She saw his concern and rubbed him lightly on the arm. "I won't. I have everything almost ready. Just a few final fittings. I can't wait. This Christmas is so special."

"That it is," Brian said, stealing a quick kiss. Mrs. Grayson pretended not to see. Blushing furiously, Bella pushed him out the door.

"Go on. Go see Reverend Franklin and come back here for your dinner. I have some presents for you to take out to Shannon and the baby," Bella said.

"Jessica will be the best dressed child in all of Wyoming. Shannon keeps talking about all these little dresses you have made for her," Brian replied before stealing another kiss.

"She's my goddaughter, I want to spoil her," Bella explained. "I have presents for Megan and Eileen too. We are invited to dinner over at their place after church on Sunday. Annie, Liam, Carolyn, and Geoff are coming too."

"What will you be like with children of your own?" Mrs. Grayson teased her.

"The best ma in the world," Brian added before he blew her a kiss and left.

Feeling warm inside, Bella opened the letter Mrs. Grayson handed her. She recognized Kathleen's letter.

"Why don't you sit down and read it. I'll make us each a cup of coffee."

"Would you like me to read it out to you Aunty Nan?" Bella teased, knowing the older woman was as curious as she was.

"Not at all, that would be nosy," Mrs. Grayson retorted. "You can tell me all about it when I sit down."

Smiling at the woman who had treated her like a daughter since she arrived and insisted she call her Aunty Nan, Bella opened the letter.

"Lily had twin boys, Laurence and Theodore. Kathleen says they call them Laurie and Teddy."

"Nice names," Mrs. Grayson said. "How is Bridget?"

"On her way back here as soon as the weather picks up," Bella answered. "Richard, Kathleen's friend, changed her medication and she is doing much better. They said they will all be here in time for Easter. For the wedding."

"Oh, Bella, isn't life wonderful? You and Brian, and Kathleen finding her young man. And Shane too. Annie and Liam can't wait to see their brother again."

Bella knew life was wonderful and she should be thankful. But part of her worried she was so happy and something bad was going to happen to spoil it.

"Stop inviting trouble, Bella darling," Mrs. Grayson said, putting a cup of coffee and a plate of cookies in front of her.

"How did you know?" Bella asked curiously.

"You have that look on your face again. You need to learn to count your blessings, dear. And we have lots of them this year."

Bella sipped her coffee. Mrs. Grayson was right, they had so many things to be grateful for. Coming to Riverside Springs had brought new opportunities. Living here in Riverside Springs had made her softer and more open to strangers. She expected to be treated better by people, and life in general, as her friends in this wonderful town had showed her over and over again how much they liked her. She had come so far from the scared girl who Kathleen had to convince to take the orphan train. She thanked God every day her friend had done that for her. She couldn't imagine living anywhere else.

Printed in Great Britain
by Amazon

49137841R00288